MURDER IS MUTUEL

MURDER IS MUTUEL

JACK DOLPH

COACHWHIP PUBLICATIONS
Greenville, Ohio

Murder is Mutuel, by Jack Dolph
© 2020 Coachwhip Publications edition

First published 1948
John ("Jack") Mather Dolph, 1895-1962
CoachwhipBooks.com

ISBN 1-61646-499-2
ISBN-13 978-1-61646-499-8

1

Painfully I hauled the seat of my pants off the floor and rolled over on my hands and knees. By the time the roaring cleared up in my head and my eyes uncrossed, Eddie Marsh was grinning like a boy at a ball game.

He said, "Upsy-daisy!"

Timmy, the gym attendant, picked me up and muttered words of comfort. "Man, whatta hook! It didn't travel six inches!" He dragged me out to the rubbing room and dumped me on a table. "You carry yer right too low, Doc. Ye'll always be a sucker for a left."

This, and similar indignities, I have suffered at the hands of Lieutenant Edward Quinn Marsh of the New York City Police Department twice each week since I got out of the service. As his personal physician, I had warned him that a man approaching forty should avoid games which took him off both feet at the same time. His feet.

As the big guy strolled into the room I noted with quite a lot of glee that there was a red area on his left cheekbone and that his lower lip was nicely swollen. He sat down on the edge of the next table and watched Timmy pull off my shoes. "Sorry I shook you up, Doc."

I said, "Don't mind me, you big flatfoot, just burn 'em in there! I'll be able to chew again in a couple of days." Timmy pulled more clothes off me and added, "Maybe you was punchin' a little hard today, eh, Loot?"

Eddie chucked his shoes in our locker. "Maybe I was, Timmy." He went off to the showers. I was annoyed by the way he brushed off my affectionate kidding.

It isn't like Eddie to be surly. We'd been casual friends for a year or so when the Harry Lennen business tangled us up and, after that, had seen a lot of each other. It was at that time, as a matter of fact, that he appointed me his personal physician, an honor which I accepted with considerable reluctance.

As it turned out, his two colds hadn't made serious inroads on my leisure and his abounding faith in whisky toddies had, on both occasions, made the treatment mutually enjoyable. By diligent inattention to my office and stalwart refusal to hire a gal for the place, I've managed to keep Eddie my only regular patient.

I suppose someday people like Marsh and, especially, a beautiful woman named Katie Storm will drive me back into general practice. So far, I like it this way.

I took a shower and went into the steam-room. The big cop was draped over the edge of a bench looking pretty down. He didn't say anything but moved over for me. When it seemed time for somebody to say something, I said, "It would be nice to know what's eating you."

"Yeah?"

"Yeah! It wouldn't be on account of knocking me on my can, would it?"

"Hell, no! That's the nicest thing that's happened to me in weeks."

"You lug."

From then on there was a long, steamy silence and I decided to let the guy sulk. About the time I began dreading the cold shower I was going to take, he said, "Where you going from here, Doc?"

"Home, I guess. It ought to be around five-thirty. Why?"

"I thought if you weren't meeting Katie or anything I'd buy you a steak."

"Are you kidding? With this jaw I eat a steak?"

"Oh. Sorry. Oysters, maybe?"

"Why don't we go back to my place and have a quiet drink? Then figure out something."

"Sounds swell. Let's go."

I cheated pleasantly on the shower and we talked Timmy out of at least half the usual manhandling and the misdirected wintergreen splashing he calls a rub. As we hit Seventh Avenue a stinging December wind took over and nobody said much down the ten cold blocks to Forty-eighth where I live.

It's a kind of a loud neighborhood and a hell of a place for a doctor's office, but it's right in the middle of all the things I like and it suits me fine. A couple of years ago, I hooked two apartments together . . . live in one and keep my tools in the other.

We rattled up in the old elevator and across the chilly hall. The apartment was a welcome warmth and the Old Forester was on the mantel where I'd left it last night. Eddie hung up his topcoat and wandered around the room looking at pictures of horses while I hustled the ice and water. I've got mostly pictures of horses, with a few ballplayers and a couple of fighters. Some of Katie, of course, and the Old Doc. Homey.

When I'd got the drinks put out and we'd settled down a little, Eddie said, "Doc, did you ever hear of a guy by the name of Panty Burke?"

I said I hadn't and what about it? Panty Burke. No. I hadn't. Panty—silly name for a guy.

"Well, if you're still interested in what's eating me, he's what's eating me."

"How come?"

Eddie took a long pull at his drink. "Well, I'll tell you. He is the guy who, for the last five weeks, has made a sucker out of me."

"Not with a left hook he hasn't. What has he done to you?"

"Among other things he's made me the laughingstock of the entire Detective Bureau. I'm supposed to find him and I can't."

"What about Missing Persons?"

"He isn't a Missing Person—I mean we want him and we haven't got him and I'm stuck with him."

"You're a detective, aren't you?"

Eddie fairly howled, "No, I'm not a detective! I'm a damned librarian. I'm a consolidator of reports. I'm an office boy for the FBI and the police of every city in America. I'm a lousy file-clerk for teletype messages! Detective, my eye!"

"You must want him badly."

"I don't want him at all, and the Department doesn't want him any more than they want a lot of people. We just can't find him and it's my case and I can't get rid of it."

"What did the guy do that makes him so important?"

"We want him for questioning about phony mutuel tickets."

So Eddie offers to buy me a steak! If it's about horses or horse racing I'm supposed to know all about it and everybody connected with it. The fact is that I do know a lot about thoroughbred horses—how they're put together and how to fix their legs when they go sore—and I know a lot of the people who breed and race them. Because of this, I know some of the people who bet and book them, but I don't give a damn for that end of it. Most people who really go for racing don't.

"Phony mutuel tickets!" I rolled that around in my head. "You can't counterfeit mutuel tickets any more. They've got a thousand ways to stop you."

Eddie put more ice in his drink. "Somebody did. We've got a lot of them. Maybe Burke made 'em, maybe he didn't. He's not around to tell us, so we think maybe he did."

"Okay, how and when did he get lost?"

"Look, Doc, if I go over this thing for you will you do something for me?"

"Like what?"

"Like ask a few questions around in places I can't get. You know every bum on Broadway."

I know it's a gag with him and I still don't like it and told him so. He grinned and jangled his ice around before he spoke.

"I'll restate it. Because of your great interest in sporting matters, and because of your unofficial position as father confessor to the denizens of . . ."

I objected to "denizens."

". . . citizens of this section, you are on speaking terms with many who . . ."

"Okay, okay. So you want me to ask the denizens what ever became of Panty." I didn't see anything wrong with that. "So now tell me about the guy."

Eddie hauled out his little black book and leaned back. From now on I'd get no kidding. On police business the man was as factual as an adding machine. "The man known as 'Panty' was William Edward Burke. He was forty-six years old, we believe, about six feet tall and weighed in the neighborhood of a hundred and ninety pounds."

I asked why the "we believe."

"No police record, no draft record. He was too young for the last war and too old for this one. Most of this came from people who'd seen him around. None of that will affect you, anyway— it's spread all over the country now. We began to be interested in Burke five weeks ago when the mutuels quietly started to talk about counterfeit tickets. The first ones had turned up at the New York tracks and later ones at Maryland. We got a tip to talk to Burke and went up to his hotel to see him—Hotel Maxton . . ."

"Stylish gent. That's for dough."

"He apparently had dough, tell you about that later. When we got there, we found he'd checked out three weeks before. That's eight weeks now. He was supposed to be headed for Florida."

"Rushing the season a little, wasn't it?"

"Not for him. He'd lived at the hotel three years and, as far as they knew, always went south around mid-October. He simply checked out as he had in the past, said good-by to the clerk and bellboys and beat it."

"Did he leave a forwarding address?"

"No. He said he'd write when he got settled. The hotel porter had bought his reservations, a section on the Seaboard, and he'd paid for them with his final bill. He left the hotel in a cab and told the driver to take him to Pennsylvania Station. Somebody occupied his section but the porter is vague about the description. We have no reason to think he did not go to Miami, maybe he didn't. We've identified him as far as the Pennsy station, but, from there on, blank."

"What else do you know about him? His life? Friends? What did he do for a living?"

"I've already told you one of the things we *think* he did for a living. As to the things we *know* he did for a living—well, he was one of what you like to call the 'percentage boys.'" Eddie smiled gently. "That's why I thought you might have known him."

I was interested enough to pass up the slur. The "percentage boys" have always fascinated me. The egg from which they are hatched is to be found wherever people live in groups and trade with one another, but their plumage and feeding habits, at maturity, are strictly environmental. In small towns everywhere, you'll find them living comfortably without any one established means of support. They'll lend you a little quick money, buy and sell anything from a couple of bales of cotton to a handful of shares in the local bank. They have few possessions of a permanent nature because such things are static. But they always have money. Money is fluid.

The genus metropolitan is an amazing creature. His coloration is protective and his feeding habits are varied, opportunistic and secretive. Contrary to Eddie's assumption that I'd know Panty Burke, they are extremely difficult to recognize. They never associate with others of their kind but feed unobtrusively among varied groups. I followed up the thought.

"One of the 'percentage boys,' eh? He must have operated a fair-sized roll to live at the Maxton."

"The management has admitted that he kept a large hunk of currency in their safe most of the time. They guess it ran into pretty serious dough, based on peeks from time to time when he opened the package at the desk."

"It had to be eight or ten grand."

"Why, Doc?"

"Figure him at a hundred and a half a week—he can make it for that kind of money. How did he live at the Maxton? What sort of a layout?"

"Nice room. Nothing fancy. Cost him ninety dollars a month."

"I didn't know you could do that up there. But it fits. He takes around eight thousand a year, and he has to have at least eight to do it." In my enthusiasm I overlooked Eddie's polite booby-trap.

"That's a new angle. What makes you think so?"

"That's the way these fellows work. They turn it over fast and safe. Fifteen or twenty moves a year . . ."

"What sort of moves?"

"Oh, maybe tickets—professional and college basketball and football seats—top-drawing fights—railroad and plane reservations to and from Florida . . ."

"Oh?"

"Sure, November and March. He needs to know somebody in the reservation end, but it works. Then you've got to consider short-time loans to people who can't afford to welsh."

"What about betting?"

"Not as a regular thing. A minus-pool show bet on a stand-out horse once in a while—a situation where the track is compelled by law to pay five or ten cents on the dollar. The 'percentage boys' aren't gamblers as such."

Eddie leaned forward and freshened up his drink. "Very instructive, Doc. I should have come to you sooner."

I was flattered. "You mean you hadn't figured those things out before?"

"Oh no. We had all that. I was just thinking I might have hit you for a couple of tickets to the Army-Navy game."

I don't bruise easily, but I get touchy about cracks concerning my invisible means of support. Neither Eddie nor Katie ever misses a cue to throw the hooks into me. They know damned well that I've got a small income. The Old Doc would never let his brother do anything for him, so he left me an annuity. Uncle Will, I mean.

"What a heel you turned out to be! You ask my help, drink my whisky and bust my jaw. . . . Now you take pot shots at my social life."

Eddie grinned happily. "Okay, pal. I'll stop drinking your whisky, now, and buy you a nice, soft, expensive dinner." He towered to his big feet and reached for his coat. "By the way. Want me to send you a list of the people we talked to?"

How can you get sore at the guy! "Sure. You might as well. If I've got to play stool-pigeon for you again I suppose I ought to know who you want me to double-cross." We were still kidding around when the thing that had been bothering me about Eddie's story came around again to the front of my mind.

"Look here, fella, there's a hole someplace in all this. What you've told me, so far, doesn't make sense."

"So?"

"Yeah. If this Panty Burke was anything like the rest of the percentage operators, he didn't have any serious connection with counterfeiting mutuel tickets. That's sure."

"How sure?"

"Five'll get you ten."

"Doc, if I had your gangster ethics instead of being a sworn enemy of the unrighteous, I'd take that bet. C'mon, let's go eat."

"What makes you so certain?"

"Facts. Nice, inalterable facts—not that 'this kind of a guy wouldn't do that kind of a thing' business."

"Such as what?"

"Such as the fact that we find part of a roll of mutuel ticket paper and some very special inks hung down the ventilator of Burke's room. Now can we go to dinner?"

2

The peerless Storm gal (Storm, Katherine Page, Smith '43—
M.A., Col. '45—unm'd—Occ.Dom.Sc.Rad. Brdcstg) is a
staunch advocate of Personal Achievement and Sterling Worth.
Unfortunately, this places me rather low on her list of persons
to be emulated. On the other hand, some charitable or mater-
nal spark plus a superb sense of humor have caused her to pay
occasional and very welcome attention to my doings. So, the day
after Eddie Marsh took me to dinner, I caught Katie's broadcast as usual, and got The Summons. When I heard her say "the
distressing habit of eating huge bowls of chile before retiring,"
I called her up. The Summons inevitably referred to one or
another of my disreputable habits.

"Hi."

"Hi." Katie sounded off at once. "Have you planned to spend
Christmas Eve in a pool hall or do you think you could wash
your face and share it with me?"

"My face?"

"You *are* an oaf, aren't you!"

"Yes, Ma'am."

"What about Christmas Eve?"

"You are the most beautiful woman in the world. I love you
very dearly. I am deeply touched . . ."

"What about Christmas Eve?"

"It's weeks away and the loneliest night in the year—unless
I can spend it with you."

"Doc!"

"I'd love it. Thanks. Where—Beekman Place?"

"No." Katie suddenly let down her guard a little. "Jimmy. I don't want Christmas at my place this year. All those stupid people . . ."

"I know, darling. I didn't have much fun last year either. What shall we do? We could go out on the town . . ."

"No." She sounded red-faced but determined. "Dammit, I don't want to make a Christmas for myself this year, or ever again."

"Will you marry me?"

"No!" Then. "No, no and *no!* But I will come over and swamp out that slovenly den of yours and make a Christmas for you."

"With a tree?"

"With a tree."

Oh Katie! Katie! Katie!

So I didn't think much about Eddie Marsh's mystery for a couple of days. I thought about neat cast-bronze signs reading James Cardigan Connor, M.D., of bossy office girls and, of course, of Katie.

I also thought, damn my perverse soul, of a blood-stirring middleweight bout which was to come up at the Garden Friday night. Johnny Constanza and Sal Lucca—a couple of local lads who had been heading for the big time in that slambang fashion the better boys—and the smarter managers—do these days.

That put me on Jacobs' Beach Friday afternoon. Jacobs' Beach? That's Forty-ninth Street, roughly between Broadway and the Garden. From the time the boys weigh in until the opening bell, you can get the prevailing odds, gossip and how's who's arthritis on Jacobs' Beach.

They liked Constanza because he was young and tough. They liked the Knickerbockers for the Saturday night basketball game. They liked the Rangers on Sunday night against the Leafs at hockey. They liked very bad cigars. They liked Constanza so much I decided against the fight and made up my mind to go home. Then I ran into Stirnie Maize.

"Hello, Doc. Takin' in the fight?"

"I didn't figure it looked too good, Stirnie, thought I'd go home."

"Yeah. Constanza should take this boy." Stirnie automatically backed up against the wall, leaning there in case the conversation should last a while. "At least there's no money around to amount to anything that says different." The little guy offered me a cigar. One of the first things you learn around there is to be wary of Jacobs' Beach favors. If you're careless about that, you learn, next, to be wary about Jacobs' Beach cigars. "I didn't think I'd go either." Maize looked at his watch. "I gotta a couple of tickets I could let you have, pretty cheap."

"Where are they, Stirnie? I might be interested."

"Fourth row ringside, Section D." He beamed. "I got 'em for myself and my wife. She couldn't make it."

I settled for the seats at a couple of dollars' profit for the guy and wondered why good fights like this one didn't sell out. It was still early enough to call Eddie Marsh and I excused myself and went to the telephone. Eddie said he would be glad to go and had I asked anybody about Panty Burke. I told him I hadn't, made a date to meet him later and rushed back to catch Stirnie. He was trying to convince somebody else it was a lousy fight but he had some tickets when I got back. I waited around. The man went away—no sale.

I said, "Hey, Stirnie. I just happened to think. There's a guy around that owes me some dough. Not a lot, but you know how it is."

"Sure, Doc. Who?"

"I wouldn't have thought much about it except that I hear he's blown town."

"Yeah? Who?"

"Panty Burke. Know him?"

"Don't you? I guess not or you wouldn't have loaned him money."

"He's that bad?"

"Burke? He's a no-good heel." Maize threw his cigar butt away as if it had suddenly nauseated him. "A no-good heel if there ever was one."

"He take you for something?"

"Him?" Stirnie chuckled unpleasantly. "Not him, Doc. I don't do business with that kind. I hardly know the guy to speak to."

"You haven't seen him around, have you?" I made it as casual as I could. The little man pulled a fresh cigar out of some inner recess, adjusted his overcoat, grinned and said:

"No. I haven't seen him around for a long time." Then: "Have you?"

They all play it wise like that and you shouldn't let it fool you. Mostly these fellows make their seedy living by knowing, or pretending to know, something obscure and valuable. A transaction involving change for a quarter is likely to bring up speculation as to what important telephone call you'll make with the extra nickel. I told Stirnie I hadn't seen Burke around. He expanded into a small, grotesque kindliness.

"Well, I'll tell you, Doc. I don't know how much dough this fella owes you, but it's ten to one against your collecting. When you heard he'd blown town, you heard right. The cops are looking for him."

"Yeah? What for?"

"I never heard what for. Could be a lot of things." He started to say something more but didn't. "Could be almost anything. He was bad."

"Was?" It couldn't hurt to try him out on that idea anyway.

"I didn't mean it that way, although I suppose there's plenty guys would like to see him out of the way for good." Stirnie hauled a pair of worn gray gloves out of his topcoat pocket. "I gotta get going, Doc. Wanta walk up to the Garden?"

We started down Forty-ninth toward Eighth Avenue, the little sharpshooter bustling along as though the destinies of the two young fighters, waiting in their hotel rooms, sat on his round shoulders. After a while he said, "No, I don't suppose anybody's killed Panty Burke. I suppose he's just got away to Mexico or someplace with a lot of dough that used to belong to a fella named Pike Manson."

"I never heard of him. Who is Pike Manson?"

Maize said, "Was."

I said, "Oh."

"Yeah, if *Pike Manson* was alive and *Burke* had disappeared, I'd come pretty close to knowing what happened. But Pike's dead, the poor bastard."

". . . and Panty Burke, you say, has his dough."

"I suppose so. Manson died broke. A bum. Broke and drunk and alone. Wait a minute, Doc, here's a guy I gotta see."

I watched Stirnie brace a couple of men who were standing at the corner. I had almost half an hour until I was to meet Eddie Marsh, and it looked like I might have at least something to tell him when I did. The three men on the corner waved arms and cigar butts with the impassioned gestures that always accompany their two-bit deals.

Broke and drunk and alone! Nice. Around this neighborhood, "broke" and "alone" are synonymous. And the kind of "drunk" that goes with these terms isn't pretty. Well, that's the sort of stuff the percentage boys leave behind them.

Stirnie detached himself from the other two and walked over to me with a broad grin. He was very pleased with himself. "They tell me Bobby Hartmann just made a good-sized bet on his boy, Doc."

"That's Lucca, isn't it?"

"Yeah. Sal Lucca. I figured this Constanza would take him but I don't want no part of any fighter Hartmann's betting against. He's the smartest manager in the business."

"So I've heard."

"Certainly don't make Constanza look like no two-and-a-half to one favorite now!" The little guy rubbed his hands.

Wonderful isn't it! I had it doped as a swell fight, an even match and a sellout. So I find Stirnie running around Forty-ninth Street saying what a lousy fight it would be and that Constanza would certainly win it. What's wonderful about it is that, all the time, Stirnie has a pocketful of tickets and a bet on Lucca! We get devious around this end of town.

"Say, Stirnie."

"Yeah, Doc?"

"What about this Pike Manson? What did Panty Burke do to him?"

"I only know what I hear and I haven't repeated what I heard to anybody. It's none of my business and I figure that knowing too much about that kind of people is a hell of a good way to get into trouble."

I agreed that he was wise and waited him out.

"Pike used to be a clerk at the mutuel windows in the days when they weren't so fussy about the help . . . followed the races around and made pretty good money. Nobody ever had anything against him and, as nearly as I ever heard, he was an honest guy. Had a pretty wife called Midge who'd been a show-girl or something. Her name was Jackson or Jansen, I forget. Maybe you heard about her."

I said I hadn't.

"Anyway, Manson quit his job with the mutuels and got into some kind of a deal with Panty Burke. Nobody seems to know much about what it was, but it must've been pretty good because they were both acting flush and hanging around the hot spots, drinking and all that. Then, a few months ago, Pike and Midge leave town quick."

"How did you happen to know about it?"

"Well, they had to borrow some money to leave on. It seemed kind of funny after all the show they'd put on. The fella they borrowed from took Midge's ring as security. That's how we learned about the rest of it."

"What's the rest?"

"Not much. They'd gone to Boston and Manson started drinking heavy and took to leaving Midge alone while he rambled around. About a month ago, while he was on one of his binges, the cops in some small town up in Massachusetts picked him up in a railroad yard. He was dead."

"How had he died?"

"Booze, exposure. I dunno. He just drunk himself to death like a lot of people." Stirnie shrugged it off. "Midge wrote a letter back and told the guy to keep the ring. I guess she's still up there."

We'd walked pretty well up to the Garden entrance and there was a big crowd around. Stirnie's gaze began to search faces so I knew he was all through with me and looking for a quick dollar again. With a pocketful of Lucca money at two-and-a-half to one, and, with the prevailing odds down close to even money, he could peddle the bet as a neat, safe profit. He couldn't be bothered with people who'd been stupid enough to die broke, alone and drunk.

I thanked him and wandered over to find Eddie Marsh. We were to meet at the bar and I ordered a Forester and water. Maybe what I'd learned would be helpful, maybe not. Manson's wife could be a source of information—and would probably talk if Burke had wrecked their lives somehow. I was mulling that over when the big cop came in. He ordered a beer.

Without informing him who'd told me, I gave Eddie the story of the Mansons, pretty much in detail. He listened gravely and drank his beer. Finally he said, "It doesn't add anything, Doc, but it was a good try. You really get around, don't you!"

I wasn't taking any bows on that. "Why doesn't it add anything? You'd think the wife would have something to say."

"She has."

"Oh. You've talked with her?"

"Look, Doc, I work for and with the greatest police organization in the world. Stuff like that is routine. Of course we've talked to her."

"What does she say?"

"She says all the right things. She says Pike Manson had a little money put away and that Burke came to him with the idea of making book. They would put their rolls together and set up a fairly sizable handbook. Manson knew the bettors and Burke knew the percentages."

". . . and that's what they did?"

"That's what Midge Manson says they did. Frankly I think it was the ticket counterfeiting business but I don't think they would have told Mrs. Manson. Whether they actually took bets or not, I'm convinced that's what she *thought* they were doing."

"I see. Then something happened and the Mansons got out of town."

"Yes." Eddie made circles with his glass on the wet bar. "The thing that happened, of course, was our investigation into the counterfeiting."

"Then why would they have had to borrow money to get out of town?"

"For the very simple reason that Pike Manson was smart enough to save his own skin by leaving Burke holding the bag."

"He didn't even stop for his money."

"That's right. He didn't stop for anything. Burke had the dough, but he also had all the incriminating stuff in his possession. Manson just left him with it. He'd been doing a lot of irresponsible drinking around town and didn't give a damn what happened anyway."

"And what did Mrs. Manson say about their running off?"

"The right thing again. She said Manson told her they'd lost some big bets and were broke and that he wanted to get out of town. On account of his drinking and his associations, she was just as anxious to move as he was."

"So they moved to Boston." It all made sense.

"So they moved to Boston. They lived in a mean little tenement apartment and, from what the neighbors say, Manson immediately began getting drunk and disappearing for several days at a time."

"Then left for good."

"Right. He disappeared in October. After he'd been gone longer than usual and his wife was worried about him, she got a letter from him asking for money."

"Oh? I hadn't learned that."

"It's all a part of the record. Manson wrote her from Middle Fairfield, a small manufacturing town in Western Massachusetts. He said he was broke and sick and wanted to come home. She sent him twenty dollars."

"Probably her last twenty."

Eddie nodded. "She says she didn't have a lot to spare, but sent him what she could. When he didn't turn up the next day, she wrote the Middle Fairfield police asking them to look around for Manson. She gave an accurate description and told them she'd heard from him there."

"So the police found him dead."

"Yes. He'd spent the twenty for liquor and, when they found him, he was lying alongside a railway embankment, obviously dead from alcoholism."

"That was the official verdict?"

"Yes. All very regular. The Middle Fairfield police notified Mrs. Manson, sent the prints to Washington and made a careful examination of the body. We checked it all because we hated like hell to lose what promised to be our best witness, or best suspect, in the counterfeiting thing. The man died from acute alcoholism. The alcohol concentration in his bloodstream was plenty to justify the verdict, even if he hadn't been lying around in the chill for something like twenty-four hours."

"So that's that."

"Just that, Doc. It's a blind lead. There's nothing there. Sorry, keed, but it was a good try. Ask around some more, will you?"

"Sure, Eddie. I might get something."

Lucca won the fight.

3

Katie called me on Saturday morning, announcing gaily that she was off for Connecticut: "the Harrisons, you know?" Yes, I knew. She sounded phony as a tout's tip and I kicked myself for not having thought up something fascinating for her week end. Maybe I'll learn, someday, that you can't take people like Katie for granted.

I scuffed out to the kitchen and put on some coffee. The prospect of a dismal week end slowed down the boiling and dried up the half grapefruit I had left from Thursday. Then the phone rang again.

"Doc?"

"Yes."

"This is Stirnie Maize." I gave him the hi Stirnie and stood by for a touch or a tip. A phone call is a nickel, so the deal had to be a dime at least.

"Look, Doc, I just happen to think of something, see?"

"Yeah?"

"Yeah. You ast me last night about that fella, the one owes you dough?" Maize waited for confirmation, so I said yeah again. "Well, I figured that maybe you had something more on your mind than collecting a few bucks."

"Why would you think that?"

"Oh, just one of them hunches a fella gets. You didn't know enough about the guy so you would have loaned him important money, and you ain't the kind to worry about small dough or a doctor bill."

It would be interesting to test the IQ of some of these big-town weasels. I'm quite certain I'd just as soon have a bet on Stirnie in the Binet-Simon Handicap as on half the business-men I know.

I laughed it off. "It isn't important, Stirnie."

"No, I s'pose not." He hesitated. "But I just happened to run into a person who could maybe tell you a lot more than I could. It so happens that this person would also like to know some things. See?"

"I see." Or, at least, I'd begun to. "But what makes you think I'd know anything that this person would like to learn, Stirnie?"

"Look, Doc. I just think it. Do I have to know why? If I'm wrong, there's no harm done. I figure both of you want to find the guy and, between you, maybe you got enough to find him with."

"Okay. Who's the mysterious person?"

"That ain't for me to say. The party will call you up if they decide to talk to you. That's up to them."

We exchanged a couple of cracks about the fight and hung up when the operator cut in for another nickel. I went back to my dried-up grapefruit and tried to figure out who Maize could have been talking about. Eddie Marsh's list was full of people I'd never heard of, and had undoubtedly been worked over plenty. It was a pretty safe bet it wouldn't be anybody in that group.

I washed the dish and the cup and took a shower. From the window, Forty-eighth Street looked particularly uninviting and I put on an old pair of corduroys and a flannel shirt. There were three or four pieces of firewood in the hall closet, so I built a fire and had just put a match to it when the phone rang.

It was Johnny Fitz asking me to help him name a yearling, a colt by Rhodes Scholar out of a good stakes mare named Seven Veils. I told him I'd go right to work on it and call him back. I like naming yearlings and quite a lot of people take my sug-gestions. Remember Bases Full? He was by a California horse called Fair Ball and an unraced mare named Three Times. Good name, bad horse.

I'd just settled down to the Rhodes Scholar-Seven Veils problem when the office buzzer sounded. A stranger. My friends didn't use that one. The office was cold as hell and I remembered I'd turned off the radiators. I answered.

"Dr. Connor?" It was a woman with a nice voice.

"Yes."

"May I see you?"

"Certainly. Come right up."

"Thank you."

I went back to the apartment and closed the office door. It had to be Stirnie Maize's "party," of course, so I waited in the hall for the elevator. When she got out I told her to come in this way as the office was cold. She thanked me pleasantly enough and went directly to the fire. My first impression was that maybe she wasn't the Stirnie party after all. This gal had a lot of poise and smelled like she was both expensive and conservative. I suggested she sit down which she accomplished without using her fanny if you know what I mean—just one neat production-piece which included thanking me, slipping her coat off her shoulders and suddenly appearing in my big chair with her legs crossed. Quality folks.

"I'm Grace Larkin, Doctor, I believe Stirnie Maize called you about me." Well, well!

"How do you do, Miss . . ."

"Miss will do." She smiled, but nice.

"Yes. Stirnie called me about you, Miss Larkin. He said you might phone."

"Perhaps I should have phoned." She took off her gloves and made a neat little pile of them on the stand beside her. "It seemed better this way. I hope you weren't busy, Doctor." Her easy glance at my costume was uncritical but it definitely challenged any attempt to say I had anything better to do.

"No. I was just loafing around. Will you have a drink?"

"A drink . . ." She looked at her watch. "Why yes, thanks, it would be very pleasant."

"Why the chronometer reading? Rules? . . . or a date?"

"Rules." She had a laugh that was worth provoking. "I ordinarily make four o'clock the deadline."

I left her warming her hands while I got the ice and stuff. Whatever this gal had to offer on the subject of Panty Burke, or whatever she wanted to know, would be worth talking about. She hadn't come up to my place to kid around. Not that one. I was curious as hell.

When I got back with the tray, she said, "This is very charming."

"Thanks. I've had some complaints about the neighborhood."

"This room is definitely not a part of the neighborhood. It could be almost anywhere." She studied the horse pictures on the wall, and there was a comfortable silence for a moment. Finally she said:

"You're very nice. I'd hoped you would be because the things I have to talk about require some understanding." She hesitated. "I suppose I should add that they also require a certain amount of . . . discretion."

"I shall try to be both understanding and discreet."

"I'm sure you will, Doctor." She lit a cigarette and leaned back in her chair. I guessed her to be in the late twenties. "Stirnie Maize tells me you are interested in finding Panty Burke."

"I am."

"So am I." The Larkin looked up at me and smiled gently, "Incidentally, Doc, before you tell me why you're trying to locate Panty Burke, let's get a better reason than that he owed you money." Just like that!

"I don't get you."

"I'm afraid you do. You see, I'm pretty much concerned as to why you're looking for Burke and I know it isn't what you told Stirnie Maize."

"What makes you think that?"

"Because the man didn't owe you a dime and because he didn't know you to speak to. He knew you by sight, as everybody else does around here." She ground out her cigarette. "I think I know why you're looking for a man you didn't know, and I don't think it will make any difference to me. But it might."

"Why do you think I'm interested in Burke, then?"

"I think you're interested in Burke because you're a friend of Eddie Marsh, the detective. Lord knows he's spending enough time looking for him, and I can't find any other reason that makes sense."

"Then why haven't you gone to Marsh for your information?"

"Now *you're* making sense." She took her hat off and chucked it on the table. "So far, for some reason, the police have seen fit to let me off lightly in their investigation of Burke's disappearance. I was questioned once about it, briefly, as a casual friend of Panty's, as were a lot of the other people he'd been seen around with. But that was all."

I didn't say anything, but wandered over to look at Eddie's list. There was no Grace Larkin among the names. At that, the list was too short to include all of anybody's casual acquaintances. Neither of us said anything for a while and I freshened up the drinks.

After a little, I said, "So . . ."

"So I'm not anxious to get further involved with the police in the matter, and I'm extremely anxious to locate Panty Burke."

"I suppose it would be out of line to ask you why you're avoiding further contact with the cops?"

"Not at all. You'd have to ask me that. Frankly, I'm afraid I might say something that would injure Panty in some way."

"You mean that you know things—of that nature?"

"That's the hell of it, Doc. I don't know if I do or not."

"I see." I believed her—it never occurred to me not to.

"I think you do see. I believe you can understand that a person needn't know anything *criminal* about somebody like Panty to harm him. As a matter of fact, I knew very little about his affairs—his business affairs."

"Of course you know that, sooner or later, I have to get around to asking you what part of his affairs you did know about?"

She looked up with that gentle smile again, a little mocking.

"We were going to be married."

Well, that's simple enough. Right on the line. She stood up with her back to the fire. Tallish with a fine pair of shoulders. The firelight made her hair redder. So Panty Burke was a heel—a chiseler and a percentage guy—and he was going to marry this girl!

I said, "That's tough. I can see why you're wary of talking to the police." I couldn't find anything around me but eggs to walk on but I took a step. "From what I hear, Burke could have been in a lot of trouble when he left."

She sat thoughtful for a moment, then she said, "From what you *haven't* heard he could have been in a lot of trouble, too."

"Police trouble?"

"No." She sat down again. "Can we skip that for now?"

"If you wish."

"Then tell me what you've heard. It *is* from Eddie Marsh, isn't it?"

I couldn't see anything to gain in being cagey, nor anything to lose for Eddie by being honest.

"Yes. There's nothing very complicated about it. The police have been looking for Burke for five weeks. Eddie Marsh thought I might have heard something. He simply asked me, and I asked Stirnie. That's all."

"I thought it might have been that way."

"The police want him for some pretty serious criminal offenses."

She looked puzzled. "Offenses?"

"Perhaps that's an unfair term . . . there haven't been any charges made against him as I understand it. Let's say they want him for questioning in connection with some serious offenses which *somebody* committed."

"I see. Will you tell me what the offenses were?"

"You don't know?"

"No."

"I'm afraid I can't tell you then, right now. I was told in confidence and I'd better keep it that way."

"All right." She finished her drink and refused another. "I suppose you're curious to know how I could be intimate enough with a man to be engaged to him and still not know why the police want him."

"Naturally. It doesn't make too much sense."

"There are two reasons, Doc. The first, and most important, is that he didn't have anything to do with the things the police are charging him with." I let that go. "The second is that he was so fond of me, idealized me so, that he refused to involve me in his life in any way until he could, well, straighten it up. He was trying to do that when he disappeared."

"How long had you known Burke?"

"Only a few weeks. I met him at a party. He was pretty attentive, and damned attractive. We went places a couple of times and then, one night at my apartment, he got serious. He told me he'd been living a useless sort of life, gambling and that sort of thing, and that he'd fallen in with a lot of people he wanted to get away from."

It was getting darker at the windows and the firelight danced softly on her face. She looked very young and very beautiful. She looked like the sort of woman any guy would want to straighten out his life for. She went on talking, and I went on believing the things she said.

"One day, five weeks ago, he came over in the afternoon and told me that he'd pretty well straightened out his affairs and was going to Miami. I knew he'd worked out a chance to go into business there, a legitimate business which would make it all right for us. What's most important is that he told me he'd wire me just as soon as he got settled. Then I was to join him. That's the last I ever heard from him."

"He didn't call you before he left?"

"No. He'd made it a point not to call me from his hotel. They keep a record of outgoing calls. He was that careful not to involve me."

Or else, I thought. The guy either was a heel, as advertised, or he'd gotten himself into something he couldn't handle. I asked her why she had told me all this when she suspected I'd been helping the cops. Her answer was simple enough.

"There was nothing else I could do, Doc. I was frantic about not being able to help, yet afraid to admit anything. Stirnie Maize, who seems to know everything, called me out of a clear sky and told me about you. He said you were fair and wouldn't let me get into trouble. I didn't even know the man but I'd heard Panty speak of him. I somehow felt that you'd be the one person who might help me do everything I can to aid Panty and to see that I don't . . . hurt him any."

I thought that over for a time. I could tell Eddie what I knew and let him, with his direct methods, get what he could. On the other hand, if her story were even partly true, I could learn a lot more than I had and still justify my indirect help to Eddie. I said:

"I'll tell you what I'll do, Grace . . ." She looked up quickly. "I'll keep what you've told me and play it your way on one condition."

"What's that?"

"It's that I don't have to defend you, or Panty Burke, to Eddie Marsh. If he comes to me with a story about you that's half as plausible as what you've told me today, I'm going to believe it."

"What sort of a story?"

"Anything that connects you directly with what Eddie's after. He doesn't make up evidence and he's fair. If he ties you up with anything off color, I'll tell him the whole thing."

"All right. I'm not afraid of that. It's a deal. In the meantime I'll bring you anything I can find. I'm scouring the town, wherever I can find anybody who was connected with Panty. That's how I learned about you from Stirnie Maize."

"Good. We may be able to dig up something between us which could help everybody concerned. There's one thing, though, that you might as well make up your mind about. If Burke is guilty, Marsh will get him."

"I know."

"You aren't afraid?"

"Not of that, no."

"What *are* you afraid of?"

"I'm afraid he's dead. I'm pretty sure they've killed him."

"Who are they'?"

"I wish I knew."

There wasn't much after that. She thanked me for the drink, left me her telephone number and went out. She was self-possessed, dry-eyed and, it seemed to me, quite wonderful.

I called up Johnny Fitz and told him to call the Rhodes Scholar-Seven Veils colt "Sabbatical."

Somewhere around seven, Eddie Marsh called up to add a name to the police list:

". . . a fella by the name of Peters . . ."

"If it's Ernie Peters, I know him." I'd met the guy around.

"Yeah?"

"Ticket speculator, the one I know."

"That's right. Ticket speculator and other things."

"What other things?" Eddie's tone suggested he'd have been disappointed if I hadn't asked. He went on:

"Former salesman and demonstrator for a check-protection company, quite an expert on inks and paper and, in general, just the right guy to know something about phony mutuel tickets." Marsh was pleased with himself.

I said, "So?"

"So he was seen with Panty Burke about a week before Burke ran out. I dug that up today. I haven't called him in and I don't intend to until I get a lot more stuff to talk to him about. I've got a hunch he's important to us and I don't want to scare him until I have something to scare him with."

"I see. And you want me to do some bird-dogging."

"Casual-like. Don't start anything."

"Okay, Eddie. I'll see what I can find out. I'm still a little sore about your cracks, though."

"What cracks, pal?" Eddie's big mouth puts his grins into his telephone voice.

"About my detecting. You call me misbeliever, cutthroat dog, and what not."

"I never . . . what the hell are you talking about?"

"Shakespeare."

"You're nuts!"

"That's what Shylock said when Antonio came around looking for some dough. He said, 'Well, now! It seems you need my help.'"

"Oh. I get it. You mean that a guy that's smart enough to know Shakespeare ought to make a hell of a detective. Okay, kid, go ahead and detect, but don't squawk to me when some tough baby starts slapping you around. Want a badge?"

"No. I want some information."

"What?"

"Did you go over Panty Burke's room for prints?"

"Of course we did . . . even if it was silly. Why?"

"Why was it silly?"

"The place had been occupied by a dozen people in the three weeks he'd been gone. Naturally there were prints, all over the place."

"Whose?"

"Everybody's. Chambermaids, the housekeeper, a parade of people from all over the country."

"Have you sorted them out?"

"Most of them. It's a mess, and I don't believe any of it's worth a damn."

"What about Burke's prints?"

"Don't be embarrassing. What do you expect? Yes. We've got some prints we think are his—there aren't any official ones, you know . . ."

"You told me."

"We think they may be Burke's because there are quite a few of them—in odd places like the under sides of things—and because we can't tie them up to anybody else."

"Any others connected with the business?"

"Yes. A lot of Pike Manson's, but they're no use to us, of course. We expected to find those. He and Burke were together a lot."

"Were there official prints on Manson?"

"There are now. The police in Massachusetts sent them to Washington. That's routine."

"So outside of Manson, who's dead, you haven't a print you're sure of to work on."

"That's right. The stuff hidden in the ventilator had been rubbed clean, nothing on it at all."

"I see. Well, thanks. I'll inquire about Peters."

Eddie sounded tired as he signed off. I don't know how the biggest police department in America manages to find so many guys like Eddie who always give it that old college try. I guess that's why they're the best in the world.

4

Next afternoon I nosed around looking for somebody who might know something about Ernie Peters. According to Eddie's instructions, I had to take it pretty easy. Finally I ran into a guy I knew as Fondi, which might be a nickname or some part of his real name. People just refer to him as Fondi.

"Ernie Peters? Have you tried Al's bar'n' grill?"

"No. Is that where he hangs out?"

"Sure. Eight' Avenyuh. What time issut?"

"Four."

"He'll be there about now. Sure he'll be there. Lookin' for basketball tickets?"

"Yeah. Thanks, Fondi. See yuh."

"Okay, Doc." The guy shuffled away on his business, whatever it is, and I headed for Al's. It's just another place, another liquor license, but they have an old man around there who buys slabs of good quality corned beef and puts them down in some mysterious solution from which they emerge as sauerbraten. I ordered some and a beer. Maybe it's because he starts with corned beef instead of an ordinary hunk of meat, I don't know, but the stuff is wonderful.

I didn't see Peters come in and when I'd finished eating I asked the old man.

"Ernie Peters? Oh, we don't see him very often. He comes in once in a while for a plate. You'd probably find him at the State Bar—that's Harry Gerber's place, you know—he's around there a lot."

I thanked him and swabbed up the gravy while he was getting my change. Fondi had better subscribe to a faster information service. The State Bar was a couple of blocks away and I didn't hurry. As I turned into the block I recognized Fondi's rusty topcoat coming out of the place and heading toward Broadway.

I might have known that, when I inquired for Ernie Peters, he would have left just a few minutes ago. Well, well! Mr. Peters didn't care to see me . . . or anybody else, probably. Eddie Marsh was right. The guy scared easily. Also, there was enough known about my interest in things and my possible connection with the police so that Fondi had ankled over there and warned Peters.

I decided to tell Eddie Marsh about that. I nickeled the phone at the State and passed it on.

"Thanks, Doc. Too bad you're losing your standing as an amateur stoolie, but it's interesting . . . and it follows the pattern."

"What pattern?" Pattern? Brother! If there was a pattern to the thing already, the police must have learned a lot of stuff I didn't know. Eddie sounded much happier than I'd heard him for a long time.

"*My* pattern, boy friend. I'm getting somewhere at last. Peters is the only guy we know around town who could furnish the savvy Burke needs to do the job he's been doing. See?"

"Yeah. So you think that, sooner or later . . ."

"Right! Sooner or later, if we don't scare Mister Peters any more, he'll take us straight to his partner." That seemed reasonable enough, if Peters were involved and somebody hadn't, as Grace Larkin feared, killed Burke. I decided to talk to Grace again and wound up the gab with Eddie talking about the boxing date we'd put off until Thursday.

I called the Larkin. "Hello, Grace, how are you? I was wondering if I could see you for a minute . . ."

"Of course, Doc . . . come over. I'm just making a cocktail. I'll make some extras." Like that.

"Thanks, I could use a drink." What am I saying! The sauerbraten rebelled, even as I spoke. "I'll be right over."

I cabbed the dozen blocks, thinking hard. I kept getting the same hunch I'd had from the first time I talked to Grace: that, somewhere, there, I'd find the answer to Eddie's mystery. I couldn't believe she knew she had it . . . or I would have taken Eddie into my confidence from the start. The gal, innocently, knew something which would be the key to the business. But to believe that, you had to believe that Panty Burke didn't get in touch with her because he *couldn't.*

She was looking very up-tempo when she let me into her rather handsome apartment. I figured she hadn't had time to set the scene since I called her . . . hence, lived pretty nicely. The cocktails were right and she'd fixed up a canape that would have been delicious if I hadn't gone for the sauerbraten.

When things got comfortably around to it, I lit a cigarette for her and asked her if she had a picture of Burke.

"No. The police asked me that. Panty was funny about pictures . . ." I told her that a lot of people were, especially if they made their livings at mildly illegal trades like bookmaking. She guessed so, too. Without resentment.

"Tell me, Grace. How anxious *are* you to find Burke?"

"That's simple enough, Doc. I want to find him more than anything in the world, if finding him won't get him into trouble."

"I see." She hesitated before she spoke.

"Why would you question my desire to find him? That's rather a strange thing to ask, after I came to you for help."

"Because I've got a hunch the answer to Burke's disappearance is right here. Either in this apartment or in your rather lovely head."

The compliment drew no fire, but the idea did. "You mean something he might have said, something I might know but didn't think was related?"

"That's right. I believe, as you do, that Burke would have gotten in touch with you if he had been able."

"I *know* that's true. That's why I've been so afraid." Either she meant it or some of our picture stars ought to take lessons from her.

"Then you'll tell me anything—everything—you can re-member? Everything whether it seems to be important or not?"

"On that basis, of course I'll tell you. I can't think of what might help."

"What was Burke going to do in Florida?"

"These." She indicated the little sandwiches. "There's a law in Miami that you can't give food away at a bar . . . and the only thing you can get to nibble on, most places, is a messy dime bag of potato chips or bad sandwiches. Panty was going to organize a company called "Flordoeuvre" to make cellophane-wrapped packages of hors d'oeuvres, fresh every day, and sold for a quar-ter." She picked up a sandwich. "This is one of his recipes."

"Cute idea." It was. But it was also small time for a guy like Burke. I said so.

"Listen, Doc, he knew that. But he also had tested the idea out and knew we could make a living at it. He didn't want any part of the big-time grift, can't you understand? That's what makes it so bad. That's what makes me so sure. Oh goddammit . . ."

"Okay, kid." I guess I patted her shoulder. "Sure. I know. That's what I think, too."

"We were going to make the damned things ourselves. We were going to buy a jeep to deliver them—doesn't that make you know he was all right?"

"Steady as you go, Gracie. We've got a lot to do and we aren't going to get any help from the cops. They don't believe that."

She straightened up and said, "Okay, Doc."

"Do you know a guy named Ernie Peters?"

She looked sick for a moment. Hurt, maybe. I don't know what she did with her face. "Yes."

"Tell me about him."

"Why are you asking me?"

"Because the police are interested in him, from *their* point of view. I want to know why—from *yours.*"

"Oh God . . ."

"You know I can't promise you a lot of things. I mean I can't help you protect Burke if he's a criminal . . ."

"He isn't! He told me that. The worst thing he'd ever done was to make book on the races. That's illegal, but not . . . what you mean."

"No. That's not what I mean. People don't disappear for good to avoid a fine of a few hundred dollars. If you believe Burke, you should have no fear of telling me about Peters."

She said, "I guess that's right."

I felt like a heel because I knew I couldn't hold out on Eddie if anything important came up. I told her so.

"I know, Doc." A nice big smile, not the brave little woman business, either. Just a nice, honest smile. "So here goes . . .

"Ernie Peters came to Panty and Pike Manson about six months ago and said that he could put them into the way of making a lot of money. That much Panty told me. Panty said it was bad business and couldn't help but wind up in a Federal rap. He told me he didn't want any part of it and that if Pike didn't quit flirting around with the idea, he was going to break up the book and get out."

"You don't know what the scheme was?" I knew, of course. So far, Eddie Marsh was startlingly right. Paper and ink expert, out of a job, comes to a bookmaker who has dough with an idea for making a lot of hot money. Then counterfeit mutuel tickets start appearing around. It's a cinch. The Larkin said she hadn't known what the scheme was. I decided to keep my own counsel.

"So far, so good. Then what?"

"Nothing. I know that Panty was worried about it. I asked him a number of times about it. He was worried about Pike Manson because Pike thought the deal, whatever it was, was a good one. That went on for some little time. Then Panty left. That's all."

"I see." At that there was some of it I could see and a hell of a lot of it I couldn't. Somebody had made the phony tickets, and somebody had made some money. If it hadn't been Panty Burke, it had to be Manson. If it had been Manson, why would he have become so broke and despondent that he'd drunk himself to death. None of it made sense unless Burke was a complete phony. Maybe he was. Certainly Eddie thought so.

I would have to report something to Eddie on Peters. I'd say I heard he'd had some sort of a deal on with Manson. I couldn't keep it all away from him no matter what I thought of Grace Larkin's story.

There wasn't much more to say and I left. On the way back I kept wondering how much the Larkin's manner and looks had to do with my ideas on the subject of Panty Burke.

As I pulled into the entrance of my place and was reaching for the key a guy behind me said, "Hello, Doc." I guess I spun around a little fast and nervous because he said, "Sorry I surprised you. I been waitin' for you."

It was one of Eddie Marsh's men. I'd seen him around. I said, "Yeah? What's up?"

The man motioned toward the street. "C'mon. I'll tell you on the way." There was a police car I hadn't noticed parked a little way below the entrance. We got in and headed for Sixth Avenue. When he'd got his driving in hand the guy said, "Lieutenant Marsh told me to bring you up to a place on Fifty-fourth."

"What for?" The fellow grinned a little on the sly side. "Boss didn't say. He just said to wait till you come home and get you t'hell up there."

At Fifty-fourth he headed east again tapping the siren once in a while. Halfway down the block there was a crowd standing around and a couple of police cars. We double-parked and I got out. A newspaper reporter said, "Hi, Doc," and the cop behind me said, "Upstairs."

It was a broken-down brownstone with an unpleasant looking basement apartment given over to stores of old rags and baled paper. I went up to the door and was sent on to the second floor. There were some cops in the hall and people going back and forth. Somebody called Marsh and he came to a door. "All right, clear this hall up! Kreutzer! See that these people belong inside or get 'em out." A cop mumbled something and started moving around. Eddie said, "In here, Doc."

I followed him back into the room and he said, "Here's your Burke case, Doc, all laid out for you." I waded through a lot

of police people, recognized the Medical Examiner's man, then
Eddie got out from in front of me.

There was a man lying dead on the floor. He had a lot of
blood on the part of his face I could see. He had an overcoat on
and his hat had come off as he fell. I didn't recognize him and
looked at Eddie.

"You don't know him, eh?"

"Not this way. Who is he?"

"There's the guy we didn't want to scare, Doc, the man you
were chasing this afternoon."

"Ernie Peters!"

"Right." Eddie pulled me off into a corner away from the
worst of the hubbub. "What time could you place Peters this
afternoon, Doc?"

I thought it out. "I went to Al's at a couple of minutes after
four. I ate a plate of food there and went straight to the State
Bar—that would be maybe half-past. They said Peters had just
left. The guy Fondi was walking out of there just ahead of me."

"Did you hang around there?"

"Not at all. I stopped long enough to make the call to you
and left."

"Then where did you go? You didn't go home."

"No, I stopped in and had cocktails with some friends." I
got a feeling I was in for an unpleasant interview and set myself
to go as easy as possible on the subject of Grace Larkin. Surpris-
ingly, Eddie changed the subject for the moment.

"Peters was shot about four-thirty. People heard it. He must
have come here straight from the State Bar. Who's this Fondi,
Doc?"

"Just a guy around. I don't know his right name or anything
about him. He's always around."

"We'll pick him up." Marsh watched a little man blowing
powder on things for prints. "It'll all be here, the whole story."

"What makes you think so?" I kept wondering about sitting with Grace Larkin—talking about what a decent guy Panty
Burke was—at the very moment when Burke must have been
shooting his counterfeiting expert in the left temple.

Eddie said, "Hell, Doc, what do you want—a blueprint? We turn the country inside out looking for Burke and nothing happens. Then we get some information on a paper and ink expert who'd been seen with him. We don't put any pressure on, much, but that sort of thing gets around. You start asking about Peters and Peters gets nervous. The first thing he does is to run to Burke's hideout. Burke shoots him and beats it. He can't get far."

"Have people around here seen him . . . can they place him?"

Eddie looked a little vulnerable on this point but blustered it out. "We're working on that. We haven't got anybody yet. There's no help in the place and the guy probably only moved at night. We'll find somebody."

"Who rented the room in the first place? You can certainly identify him." I thought I'd made a point.

Eddie pointed to the body. "Peters rented it."

The little guy with the print powder came over to us. He nodded at me as though he knew me. Eddie said, "What about it, Harry? Can you make a guess?"

"I don't have to guess, Lieutenant. They're all over the place. I'd know 'em anyplace—I spent enough time with 'em."

"No question of their matching?"

"None whatever. I'll show you when we develop the films."

"Good. Thanks, Harry. We'll need the actual comparisons fast, so get going." The little guy went about packing up his stuff and we just stood there for a moment.

I said, "That makes it Burke, eh?"

Eddie said, "Who else?"

So there it was. All neat and clean. Eddie Marsh finds Panty Burke and electrocutes him. Just like that . . . and so I am a chump . . . and so I don't believe it . . . and so, currently, I am lying in a rented Fowler hospital bed with my left leg in a traction splint, typing on a beautiful new invalid's table which cost Katie $47.50 at Macy's.

5

I called Grace Larkin back that night. She was pretty panicky
when I told her about Peters, and asked me to come over. I
thought I'd better go because I wasn't going to be able to hold
out on Eddie Marsh for her much longer. She'd been eating
some sort of a salad but had left most of it. I suppose my phone
call had fixed that. When we'd got settled down, I said:

"It doesn't look so good, does it!"

She bit on a knuckle. She was in bad shape. "I can't understand it, Doc. There's something terribly wrong."

"I'll say there's something wrong!" There wasn't any halfway
measure I could think of. You couldn't soften it up much. "The
thing that's wrong is that it looks like your guy never intended
to go to Florida. It looks like he's been in New York all the
time."

"I don't believe it."

"How can you believe anything else?"

"He would have gotten in touch with me someway."

Maybe. "Not necessarily. He'd be exposing you to what now
appears to be a lot of trouble." I was convincing myself. "He
must have been in a jam, something to do with Peters, and had
to do it this way."

"I still don't believe it." She opened and closed a metal compact. Her finger shook a little. "I . . . I'm sorry . . ." She got
up and went into the bathroom. I heard water running and sat
around waiting. I found an old blank in my pocket and wrote a
prescription for a sedative.

After a little while she came back looking rather handsomely bedraggled. She said, "I'm sorry, Doc."

There wasn't much to do and I told her so. "The cops are going to ask you a lot of questions, Grace. You'd better answer them the best you can. It isn't a matter of getting Burke into trouble now. He's in all the trouble there is anyway."

"Then, if they ask me, you think I should tell them about Ernie Peters?"

"Certainly." I got nervous and started walking around. "What is there to gain by making yourself look bad? Look. The guy got himself into a spot where he had to stop Peters. He's in plenty trouble and he doesn't want you in it. Peters lost his nerve and became a bad threat to Burke's safety. It was either Peters or Burke and Panty played it the only way he knew how."

"Okay, Doc, I guess you're right." The Larkin started pacing, too. We were walking around the apartment like a couple of Englishmen on a liner. She stopped. "Doc. Tell me this. Do they *know*—the police, I mean—do they *know* that Panty shot Peters?"

I looked at my watch and decided Eddie would be at his office. I said, "Wait a minute," and called. They got Eddie on the line and he was all business. I knew he'd been answering a lot of phone calls by the way he snapped "Marsh" at me.

"Doc, Eddie."

"Yeah, Doc?"

"On the Peters business. Is there any doubt in your mind who shot him?"

"None whatever. I'm asking immediate in absentia indictment for murder. When we find Burke he's a dead duck." Marsh left no doubt any place. "Your friend Fondi knew Peters was in some sort of trouble with Burke and told us he'd seen them together months ago. When he told Peters you were looking for him, Fondi says Peters was scared as hell. To use your favorite expression, it all makes sense."

"I suppose so. But look here, Eddie, wasn't there some question about the fingerprints? You actually haven't got a set of Burke's prints, have you?"

"Listen, sonny. I'm not doing any worrying about Burke's prints as long as Burke keeps the same fingers. I've got the prints of the guy who killed Peters and I've got the prints of the guy who lived in Burke's apartment and when I find Burke, those are the prints he'll be wearing. Whaddyah want, pictures?"

I said I guessed not and hung up. Grace Larkin asked me if I'd have a drink and I told her I would. She brought out some Scotch, which I dislike, but accepted. As she brought in the ice, she said, "From your conversation I judge the police believe Panty killed Ernie Peters."

"Yes. They're asking an indictment."

"What was that about fingerprints?"

"It's not open to question." I told her what Eddie had said. I also told her that Marsh seemed so positive of his ground that she might not be questioned too much but would probably be watched. She just sat there and didn't say anything.

I fooled around with my drink for a while because I couldn't think of anything to say, either.

Then the phone rang. Grace looked startled. She got up and moved toward the stand where the instrument was. It rang again and she answered.

"Yes . . ."

She pressed the receiver close to her ear but I could catch the raspiness of a voice . . . no words.

"I . . . please! I . . . all right, go ahead."

The mumbling went on steadily for some time. Grace looked so sick and frightened that I started over. She looked at me with such naked horror in her eyes that I reached out my hand toward her. She leaned away, shielding the phone from me.

The mumbling stopped. The girl dropped the receiver and it slid off her lap to the floor . . . then she slid off her chair after it and I grabbed her as she fell. By the time I'd got my ear to the phone I heard only the dial tone.

I carried Grace into the bedroom, stretched her out and threw a quilt over her. She moaned her way back to consciousness and looked pretty green. I got a wet towel from the bathroom and got it back in time for her to vomit.

Pretty soon I said, "All right, now?"

She said, "Yes . . . I guess so . . ."

"What happened?"

She groped with something for a while as she fought her way out of the dopiness. "I don't know," she said. I decided to wait and let her straighten herself out while I cleaned her up a little. She seemed grateful for the cool towel on her face.

"Do you think you'd hold a drink down? You need one."

"I think so. Yes. I think so."

I went out and poured a stiffish slug of the Scotch, diluted it a little and poured it down her. When it looked like the drink was going to stick, I said, "Now can you tell me what happened?"

She tried to sit up and I told her to stay down some more. She avoided looking at me. "Would you mind going home now, Doc?"

"Not while you're this way . . . and not until you tell me what's wrong. Who was that called you?"

"I'd like it if you left, Doc. There isn't anything I can say."

"Is someone coming here?"

She looked terrified. "No. No! I just want you to go."

"All right, Grace, if you want. I'm not the cops, you know. They'll find out about it. It's none of my business. I won't ask you any more questions. I'd like to help you if you'll let me."

"You can't. Thanks. I don't need anything."

"You need sedation. Got any nembutal or anything?"

"There's something in the medicine cabinet. I guess that's what it is. It says one at bedtime . . ."

I said, "One at bedtime, if necessary . . . that'll be it." I went out into the bathroom and looked into the cabinet. I took a good look, partly because I couldn't find the prescription right away. After I'd found it, I ran the water but kept looking. Among other things was a Rolls razor!

Now you can find almost any sort of a razor among a lady's gear, but one of the kinds you *don't* find is a wedge-bladed, self-honing Rolls. It's one of these demonstrate-with-pride jobs for guys who love beautiful steel. It was sort of back of other stuff and I picked it up and looked it over. It had been used considerably and had a film of shaving soap here and there. Apparently it had not been used for some time and relegated to the back of the cabinet. It had to be Burke's, of course. I turned it over. Right in the middle of the bottom was as pretty a thumbprint as you ever saw. I said, "Oh here it is," and put the thing into some layers of toilet paper and shoved it into my coat pocket.

The medicine was nembutal and I carried two and a glass of water out to Grace. "These'll help some."

"Two?" She looked quite serious about it.

"Why not? You've taken them before, haven't you?"

"Yes. But I . . ." The girl shuddered a little.

"You what?"

"I don't want to go to sleep!"

I thought that over as I told her she wouldn't necessarily go to sleep in her state and gave her the pills. By that time I wanted to get away. She thanked me without smiling.

"I'd rather you forgot about my problems now, Doc. You say you're not the cops and that it's none of your business. All right then . . . please, please, Doc, *don't* be the cops. There isn't anything more I can tell you, and, there isn't anything more you can do for me. Will you play it that way?"

That took a little study. When I'd got my mind made up, I said, "Eddie Marsh asked me to see if I could locate Burke. I inquired around and didn't get any place. Then he asked me to see what I could learn about Ernie Peters. Ernie Peters is dead. Burke apparently either killed the guy or had been in the room with him when he was killed."

Grace Larkin didn't budge as I watched her. I went on:

"Now Eddie has a murder case, a victim and Burke all set up in normal routine police order. He knows about that sort of thing and I don't. The only thing I know about you that Lieutenant Marsh doesn't know is that you got some sort of phone call today that scared the hell out of you. I'm not going to try to slap information out of you and I'm not going to help Eddie do it. From now on, the case is his. That suit you?"

She smiled. "Thanks, Doc."

I got my hat and coat and beat it. As I went out the entrance I had half a hunch I'd see Burke snooping around but I didn't. There was a big guy standing smoking a cigarette across from the doorway. Just for curiosity I walked down the side of the building to the alley—the only other entrance. There was another big guy standing there smoking another cigarette. Any need I had thought I might have had for reporting the possibility of Burke's being in that neighborhood vanished. Eddie hadn't neglected the neighborhood.

I went home without conscience trouble.

After I'd gotten settled down with a mild Old Forester I hauled out my prize and tried to figure out what to do with it—a lovely, clean print in dried soap. Probably the only right thing to do was give it to Eddie. Actually he didn't need it and I didn't want to start anything for the Larkin. Eddie had plenty of Burke's prints by now. All he needed was Burke.

A second, and rather stronger Forester, put me in an experimental mood. I'd do a little research on my own. I got some after-shave powder and sprinkled it on a piece of paper. I carefully blew the stuff on the print and blew it off again. There it was, all sharp and strong. The cops couldn't have done better.

Next, my little German camera. I set it up in the office under my big light and made half a dozen shots of the print. It was late, but I knew Johnny Patch up the street would be working and I headed up there. Johnny has the sort of a place where sailors get their pictures taken in a property buggy or with aprons, standing behind a phony bar."

"How's business, Johnny?" There wasn't a soul in the joint.

"Great, Doc . . . that is, unless you want a loan."

I told him it was a touch, all right, but not that kind. He took the film and told me to watch the place as he went back to the darkroom. I stalled around. Nobody came in. It started to sleet.

After a while Johnny came out from the back wiping his hands.

"You may be a good doctor but you're a lousy photographer."

"What's the matter? Are they all bad?"

"No. A couple of them are fair." Johnny grinned. "Whatcha doin' now, Doc? Workin' for the cops?"

"No. I'm doing a study on the thumbprints of identical twins."

Patch gave me a funny look and scratched his head. "If you'd of said horses I would've believed you. Want prints of all of 'em?"

"Just the cleanest one. Two, three prints. Can you make them tonight?"

"Tonight! I take this stuff and deliver it in an hour . . . lots of times, less." He went back to the rear again. It wasn't long until he brought me the prints, quite dry. They looked very official.

At home, again, I studied the whorls and the gimmicks and pondered over the insignificance of the things which make the difference between men.

6

Next day I wandered into Rosie's about eleven with my mind on hot cakes and sausage. There wasn't a stray newspaper at any of the tables, so I sat at the counter. Rosie asked what would it be and I remembered I had a gymnasium date with Eddie in time to order boiled eggs, dry toast and tea. If you think that sounds silly, you should take a few of Eddie's short rights to the middle.

I thought about my thumbprints, stowed carefully in my wallet and making me curious. I could ask Eddie to bring up Burke's prints when we met this afternoon. I could just send him up to raid the Larkin's place, too. I'd have to tell him where they came from.

Rosie said the streets was sure a mess and I said yes they were . . . after I remembered they were. She had a cold and asked me what to do about it. I told her to quit serving food to people, which was a mistake, because I let myself in for a long lecture on how she maintained her standards of public hygiene with a runny nose. I thought about needing a medium-weight topcoat. It was that kind of a morning. There didn't seem to be enough to do.

I finished my breakfast and left. On the way back to the apartment I picked up a paper and some cigarettes. The walks were icy and people were chipping at them with things. They made small, ineffectual ringing sounds. I wondered where Panty Burke was. Probably lying in some dirty hole sweating it out. Probably cursing a schedule which had brought him Grace

Larkin when he was too badly involved with the law to get out
without having to shoot somebody.

As I got out of the elevator on my floor I was greeted by an
open door, buckets and a mop. Thursday! Mrs. Parter—open
windows, noise, gab and that damned vacuum-cleaner! I tried
to sneak in the office way and banged the door against her fat
old fan.

"I'm moppin' here now. You'll have to go the other way."
I said I'd come back later. She hollered back, "You're to call
Mister Marsh before you go 'way." I went into my inhospitable
living quarters, dumped a lot of dirty sheets off my chair and
called Eddie.

"Look, Doc; no gym today. I'm busy."

"That's the last straw. My damned apartment's full of clean-
ing woman and I haven't anything to do."

"Go up and box with Timmy."

"Are you kidding? I'd kill him. What's the matter with you?"

"There's stuff all over the place . . . I'm swamped,"

"Filing teletypes again?"

"Hell, no! We got action!" Eddie laughed. "Hey! I'd forgotten *you* were detecting on the case. You can close the file, kid."

I said, "Why?"

"We've got the guy right this time. He blew out of his hole
so fast the other night he left a lotta stuff behind. We got him
sure, now. He can't get out of town."

"What sort of stuff did he leave?"

"Plenty! A lot of his old records, bookmaking records of his
deals with Pike Manson. Old stuff with Manson's prints on it
as well as his. All in a metal box with *both* Burke's prints and
guess whose on it?"

"Whose?"

"The corpse's. Peters'! Nice?"

I said yes, it was nice.

"Conclusive?"

I said yes, it was conclusive. We agreed to try the gym date
again the following Tuesday. Eddie thought it would be over by

that time. Neither of us remembered that Tuesday was Christmas Eve and guys had no business slugging each other around on Christmas Eve.

The thought of Christmas cheered me up a lot because I could go out and get things for Katie. The sight of Mrs. Parter making with the mop was suddenly a fine thing and I told her to give it hell, that I was having visitors. I gave her five bucks extra.

Eddie had his case and I was just fresh out of detecting. I took the fingerprint pictures out of my pocket and chucked them into a drawer. I couldn't see what good it would do to let Marsh know that Burke had lived with Grace Larkin instead of just knowing her. I decided not to try to return the razor.

When Mrs. Parter started overhauling the living room, I got out and headed east. Katie's not easy to buy things for and I knew I'd better keep it pretty conservative. A cab driver was standing in Rosie's doorway, picking his teeth. I got into the cab and he followed.

I said, "Georg Jensen's."

He said, "Yeah?"

There wasn't any reason for his saying, "Yeah?" that way and I got sore. "Would you like me to go someplace else?"

"No. I just always get a laugh outta he's got no e on his Georg."

"That's Danish."

The dope laughed like hell. "I like 'em with coffee." What can you do with a guy like that? When he let me out at Jensen's he said, "Merry Christmas, Doc." I looked up from making change and he added, "I hauled you lots of times."

Just in case it had been some of the special times I tipped him half a buck and retreated into the store. Forty-five minutes later I emerged into the cold again with my pores all open and clutching the most beautiful serving tray I've ever seen, a Jensen original, and, mister, there aren't too many around and whoever priced the piece knew it. Katie loved silver and I'd given her a couple of smaller pieces of the same design before. I was practically broke and happy as guys ever get.

On the way back I stopped at the liquor store and ordered some champagne. Funny, I've been around people who said they knew about wines and vintages and things all my life but I've never absorbed any of the lore. It was a good store and the man said it was the best he had. I wrote him a check and made a mental note to send out some bills in January. I do sometimes.

When I got to the apartment entrance there was a Christmas tree standing in the entry. A guy peered out through the branches and said, "Are you Dr. Connor?" I helped him lug the tree into the elevator and up to the apartment. It had a good, professional bottom on it and stayed where it was set. The man said there was no charge, so I tipped him and stood off to admire the tree. It was a Fifth Avenue tree and probably very expensive. Katie never did anything halfway.

The guy rattled down in the elevator and Mrs. Parter came in from the office with the laundry bags. She had her hat on and, I paid her the regular fee. When she'd gone I turned on Katie's show. She was in fine fettle and, among other things, gave me The Summons. It had to do, this time, with . . . "taking part in a movement, this year, to see that some of the lonely and homeless men of the overcrowded and less reputable sections of the city could share in the joys of Christmas." One tree, in fact, she had sent on its way just today.

I called her up.

"Do you know where to set it?" She didn't wait for an answer. "Put it right in between the windows. You'll have to move the desk, but that's light and can go anywhere. Did the decorations come?"

"Not yet. I bought the champagne."

" . . . the decorations will be there from Macy's sometime today. Will you be there?"

I said I supposed I would and tried to tell her about the champagne again . . . and, altogether, felt pretty overwhelmed. I guess Christmas gets that way in families. It's kind of discouraging.

Katie went on. "There are a few small things I'd like to have you get. I'll give you a list. Also I think you'd better leave me the key, someway."

"I've been trying to give you one for years."

"I haven't got time to tell you what a heel you are right now, so listen. Will your oven hold a turkey?"

"Turkey? I never . . . I mean . . ." Maybe that isn't what I said but it probably sounded that way.

"Never mind. I'm roasting it at home. I just wanted to keep it hot. We'll do that on top of the stove if necessary. I'm bringing everything on Tuesday and I'll want you to help. Right after my show."

"Should I be making notes?"

"You should be making sense. Tomorrow's Friday and I've got stuff to do besides my broadcast, so I can't trim the tree until tomorrow night. Will you be there?"

"Of course. Will we have dinner?"

"No. It's the office party and I'll eat more than I should because the stuff is always so good. I'll be there after dinner time. Right?"

"Right."

"Okay. Now, darling, thanks for buying the champagne which you told me twice. You are a very sweet guy and I love you dearly. Be sure to be there when the decorations come. Good-by, Jimmy."

Oh Katie! Katie! Katie!

Christmas sort of set in, then, and I ordered a lot of wood for the fireplace and made a list of people I'd rush cards to. The man came with the decorations, a huge package, and the liquor-store man brought the champagne. Stuff was happening all over the place.

The buzzer sounded off again and in a few minutes. I unlatched the door. Eddie Marsh was getting out of the elevator. He looked serious as hell.

"Hello, Doc. Can I talk to you a while?"

"Sure, Eddie. Come in." He shouldered his way through the door and looked around the room. He didn't say anything about the Christmas tree and I knew something was wrong.

"Take off your coat. Have a drink?"

"Thanks. No. I'd better not." He tossed his coat down and looked at me with a kind of tired grin. I told him to sit down and he did. In a minute he said, "Doc, I want to know what's become of Grace Larkin."

I did a little fast thinking and said, "Grace Larkin?"

Eddie ran his hand over his face. "So it's going to be that way!"

I said, "What way?"

"That way, dammit. Like everybody else I have to ask questions of. I tell you I need to know what's become of Grace Larkin and you give me that stuff. I take it for granted that I don't have to kid around with you, that I don't have to be a cop with you, and you ask me who Grace Larkin is! You were there last night, weren't you?"

"Yes. I was."

"Okay. I know what time you went there and when you left . . ."

"I saw your men."

"Tell me what happened." Eddie sounded uncomfortable and I guess he was. I knew he'd put the pressure on me if he had to. He knew I knew it, too. "I'm not asking you why you went there, Doc. You had enough knowledge of the Burke case to go there, and probably enough of your old amateur sleuth yen in you to want to. I just need some facts."

"You say she's gone?"

"In the night. I had men on the place but she got out. It wouldn't have been too difficult. The men move around some on a cold night. She didn't take much with her, that's sure. Maybe a small bag."

"What do you want her for?"

"I find, now, that she was Burke's girl. Burke's in New York. I'd counted on her to lead us to Burke . . . or that he'd try to see her. What did she tell you?"

I said, "I'll tell you, Eddie, if I'd thought any of the stuff she told me would have helped you, I'd have given it to you."

"I feel pretty certain you would." Then he added. "Not that you'd have much of an idea about what's worth anything to us."

"I felt sorry for the Larkin girl. She'd taken an awful beating from Burke." I told him everything the Larkin had told me, even about the Flordoeuvre thing. I told him about the phone call and he didn't seem too excited although I expected he'd raise hell.

"Burke called her, of course. I couldn't tap her phone."

Then I told him about the Rolls razor and he laughed in spite of his lousy mood.

"I don't suppose your information would have made any difference, Doc, except the call. I would have done something about that. Well, hell! It's not the first time you've got in my way, kid." Then he laughed again. "So you snooped around and got a print. Got it here?"

I told him I had and dug the pictures out of the drawer. Eddie looked them over and said, "Very professional. I'll get you a badge." He shuffled around in his breast pocket and came up with some papers. Then he grunted a couple of times and got up and lumbered over to the light. He said, "I'll be damned!"

I asked him what it was.

"You've got this razor?"

I brought it out and he studied the thing carefully. "And you found it well back in Larkin's medicine cabinet, like it was not in use regularly?"

"That's right. Prescriptions and stuff like that in front of it. As a matter of fact, it was so well hidden I thought she wouldn't miss it herself."

Eddie said he'd be damned again and I asked him what was wrong. He had a funny look on his face.

"Nothing's wrong, pal. A very nice job of snooping, and not too bad a job of print-taking. I really will get you a badge."

"What goes? Have I solved your case or something?"

"Oh no! you're not that good, but you've just added a cute touch to the Larkin saga."

"How?"

"You've just proved the little lady to be a double-crosser and a tramp . . . and, very possibly more."

"Great! How did I do all that?"

"You named the guy with whom she was living, or damned intimate with, during what must have been the time of all the counterfeiting deals with Peters, during the time Burke was doing the courting and she was giving him the sweet meet-you-in-Florida talk."

"You mean the print isn't Panty Burke's?"

"Hell, no!" Eddie was very pleased with himself. "This print was made by the guy they shoved out, the guy they robbed, the guy who went off and drank himself to death on account of what they did to him!"

"Pike Manson!"

"Exactly!" said Eddie. "Now I'll have that drink with you."

7

It snowed all day Friday and Katie came over around six, loaded with bundles and several of the office-party cocktails. Anyway, she was bouncing around.

She gave me a fast, show-businessy kiss and dumped all the stuff on the couch. I'd moved the tree in between the windows and unpacked the decorations. The fire was going nicely and it looked pretty homey altogether. Katie took off her coat and hat and I hung them up. When I came back she was standing in the middle of the room with her hands on her hips looking at the tree.

"All right, isn't it!" She looked over her shoulder in a way she has . . . without turning around at all. I told her it was wonderful and how much I loved her. She said, "Quiet, oaf, I'm thinking about where to put what on it. You'll have to break that topknot off a little so the star can go on." She went over and dug around in the stuff and pulled out the star. "Get a kitchen chair and we'll see what goes."

I got the chair and put it in front of the tree. Katie dragged over the string of lights that went with the star and climbed up on the chair. To see her climb up on a chair would have made Flo Ziegfeld reach for a contract. I said, "Fascinating!"

"Get your mind on the business at hand, you adolescent. Help me get this damned cord untangled. It's caught in the branches . . ."

That sort of thing went on for a long time. When all the lights were strung we tested them and got to work on the rest of the stuff, all sorts of very fancy gags for the branch tips and colored balls for the inner places. It was pretty good fun until we had put in what seemed like an hour hanging drips. I was for throwing them on but Katie explained, several times, that the delicacy of the whole thing depended on their being placed on one at a time. It made a lovely effect, I had to admit, but it was a hell of a chore.

I gave it up, finally, and mixed myself a drink. It was all pretty beautiful and I got a little maudlin while Katie kept hanging up the stuff and backing away and looking. About ten o'clock she sent me for a broom and we straightened the floor up.

"Now," said Katie, "I'd like a drink and some food."

"Where?"

"Anywhere the drinks are good and the food is at least pretty good." Katie brushed herself off and started to put her things on. "It ought to be some place we can talk, too."

"You know me, Babe. When you talk over a dinner table what would I want of a floor show?"

"I'm not talking, and don't call me babe. You're talking and I'm listening."

"About which?"

"About the Great Panty Burke mystery, about the murder of a man named Peters and, mostly, about your visiting beautiful trollops by the name of Larkin." She was very explicit. "What's worse, having them here in your . . . den."

I was somewhat taken, as they say, aback. "What are you, a secret agent?"

"I'm a reasonably intelligent woman and I read the papers."

"That's not enough . . . at least unless . . . hey! The Larkin business isn't in the papers, is it?"

"Not your part of the escapade. In all fairness I probably should have said that I meet your friends on the street once in a while."

"So Eddie Marsh's been putting you up to needling me!"

"I met him this afternoon. He did mention that you might have some things to confess."

"Okay, my lamb. Things will be confessed. What about the neighborhood? What about Gallagher's?"

"Am I that hungry?"

"Remember our last meal there? Think it over. Steak burned on the outside and raw in the middle, hashed-brown potatoes, half a head of lettuce with Roquefort dressing?"

Katie said, "I'll go quietly," and we galloped out. We stopped and looked at the steaks in the window when we got there. To see the care they take of the stuff sort of numbs you for the check. I know a lot of guys around there—I mean guys who spend their odd hours at the bar—and I said hi a couple of times as we went in. The girl at the checking place said, "Good evening. Doctor. We don't see you much any more."

Katie said, "That's good," and we followed the captain back to a table.

We kidded our way through a couple of martinis and a tremendous lot of wonderful food before we got to the Burke business. I told Katie the whole thing as carefully as I could. You can't tell the Storm gal anything any other way if she's interested. She makes you stop and go back.

When I got through, she said, "It isn't a very pretty story."

"I don't suppose that sort of story ever is . . . just a lot of wrong people doing a lot of wrong things."

Katie finished appraising the fiftyish gent and the would-be debutante someplace at the next table, without comment. Then she said, "I don't mean that. A lot of wrong people do a lot of wrong things more interestingly than that, not always so sordidly."

"You figure it's just that simple."

"Yes. Of course. It's the commonest story in the book—a double cross with a woman in the middle."

"A two-motive double cross—love and money . . ." Katie looked at me full of fight. "Love my foot! If that's love I'll get along without it."

"You don't believe Burke wanted to get out."

"Sure he wanted to get out," snapped Virtue Rampant. "He wanted to get out with all Pike Manson's money, Pike's mistress and a nice, clean bill of health from the police."

" . . . and so Grace Larkin didn't love him . . . Burke?"

"Love him? Sure she loves him . . . or she did before he killed Peters. He has the dough, hasn't he?"

"That way, eh?" Katie annoys me sometimes when she gets tough. What's more, when she finds out she's annoying me, she keeps it up. "Grace Larkin seemed like quite a lot of woman to me."

Damned if she didn't leer! It looked awful on that lovely Irish map. "Grace Larkin has apparently seemed like a lot of woman to a lot of guys."

I said listen here or something.

"Look, you Broadway Lancelot! Pike Manson and Panty Burke are partners in a bookmaking business. Pike has some sort of a wife. He also has a mistress

named Grace. He leaves his razor around her place and she doesn't even bother to hide it when she entertains her lover's partner. Pike's a piker, a softie. Make sense, so far?"

"I suppose so." It did. It made nasty sense.

"Now!" I don't think I'd ever seen Katie's claws before, but I suppose all dames have them. "Now! Burke gets into a deal with Ernie Peters to make phony mutuel tickets. As I say, Manson's a sissy. He won't go into it. Grace Larkin likes the deal and takes on Burke . . ."

I hollered. "Dammit, Katie, don't talk that way! It's not nice . . . it sounds tough."

She gave me that big Irish grin, guileless as hell and beautiful as cherubim and seraphim. "All right, darling. I was only trying to express it so you could understand me. You talk that way."

"I don't anything of the kind!" But I couldn't put my heart into it. I can't take that grin. I smiled back and said, "Okay, go ahead."

"All right. Grace Larkin gets in with Burke and, between them, they scare Manson off—and break his heart in the bargain. Manson gets out of town with his unsatisfactory wife and goes on the rocks. The unsatisfactory wife is paying five dollars a week or something on his headstone."

"It isn't pretty, is it!"

"No. It smells. Meantime, Burke is getting ready to go back into business with Peters when you come galloping along and scare the counterfeiter by prowling around town after him. Peters loses his nerve, Burke loses his head and shoots him. Burke calls Grace Larkin on the telephone and scares her out of town."

That didn't seem to fit, that scaring his mistress out of town, and I said so.

"If you mean that the Larkin woman has run off to meet Burke some place, you're plain crazy. Not that one. Burke undoubtedly wanted her to, and suggested it over the phone. You can bet he did that. But you can also bet that his girl friend has gone just as far as she can get in the other direction. She's playing it strictly for Larkin and not for what you quaintly call Love."

Well, I couldn't figure out anything better to offer. It fit with all the facts—Manson's old prints in Grace's bathroom, Burke's new ones on the box that he left where Peters was killed. Peters' fresh prints on the same box put them together, probably in that room. It was pretty hard to get around Katie's statement of the case. It would be Eddie Marsh's case, too. Katie was gathering up her stuff.

"Soooo . . ." she said, "we'll have a nice quiet Christmas and you can forget all about the Burke case. You can forget all about the beautiful Larkin, too."

"I suppose so." I hauled out my wallet. "You could have fooled me . . ."

"Anybody could have fooled you, Jimmy my darling. I've been getting away with it for years."

"Yeah?"

"Yeah. Shall we go?"

We went. I exchanged pleasantries with the doorman for half a buck and we took a cab across town to Katie's place. I guess we were tired or something because we didn't say much on the way. At her apartment house entrance I held her hand for a minute or two while we said things about Christmas. Then she spoke very softly . . .

"It's fun to make plans, Jimmy."

"Isn't it!" Sometimes I can't look at Katie's eager beauty without dreaming dreams which would probably end up by making us both unhappy. I dreamed them then. "Hell, sweet, I wonder . . ."

"So do I . . . sometimes."

"Do you? Really?"

"Oh yes. So often. Oh, darling, so terribly often. I wonder if we aren't both getting . . . oh sort of tough and wise-guy . . . sort of phonyish . . ."

"There's a lot of it around, isn't there!"

So much of it in my end of town. Maybe a good deal of it in hers, too, in a different way. There are lots of ways for people to get phony. I said, "You know how I feel . . . you know that if I thought it wouldn't throw us both to try to adjust our . . . I can't say *work*, can I!"

The cab driver lit a cigarette and turned off the motor. Katie smiled. "Jimmy, I don't even know if I'd love you at all if you were—respectable. That scares me. I might not love you in the same way. And I don't want to love you any other way . . . except this."

That did it. I held her in my arms and felt her sob. I knew that when that moment was over the cab driver could step on the starter.

8

Saturday morning the papers carried the whole story, a roundup yarn in which Eddie came off pretty well on top. He had been as cautious as usual in his statements, but gave the impression that the case was wrapped up and that the apprehension of Panty Burke seemed to be a matter of hours. Marsh had tied the whole association of Burke and the murdered Peters together with the rather astonishing statement that Peters had been the man who had occupied Burke's Florida-bound compartment. The porter had finally identified photographs.

So, for reasons of their own, Burke had stayed in New York and Peters had gone on ahead to Florida. Nothing out of line, it seems, there. Nothing much was said about Grace Larkin except that she had not been located and was wanted for questioning.

I tried to dismiss the whole thing from my mind. Katie's cold analysis of the Larkin woman had been based on facts and an objective viewpoint. My resistance to believing that sort of thing about her was based on my personal contacts with her, and the fact that I am probably a sucker for people, women especially, with nice manners. She had apparently fooled Manson and Burke in turn, no reason why she couldn't have taken me in as well.

I walked up the street through the nasty day and stopped in at the Cecil Tavern. It's a little off the beat—I mean the fight and horse crowd doesn't get over there—and I like to talk to Julius. When he saw me he gave the glad cry and whipped out the Forester.

"We have seen too little of you, Doctor. Have you been away?"

I told him I hadn't been away and settled down on one of his high stools to nurse my drink along. Jack, the bartender, came in and they discussed the details of the day. Something kept nagging at my mind. I sorted out the things Grace Larkin had said to me at my apartment, things she'd said the night Peters was killed.

"We were going to be married." "I knew very little about his business affairs." "I'm pretty sure he's dead. I'm pretty sure they've killed him." I must have sat quite a while.

Julius gently suggested another drink. I said yes and asked him if he believed a man should play his strong hunches. He thought it over while he made the drink.

He's a very serious guy and something of a philosopher.

"Mostly I should say yes, Doctor. With you, yes. With a lot of people, no."

"What's that mean?"

"It is my opinion that hunches are convictions which are formed unconsciously from things we already know."

"Intuition, Julius."

He spread his hands. He's continental, British and American all mixed up. "If you like, yes. The hunch of an experienced and honest horseman is often a good bet, is it not?"

"I see your point. He has unconsciously put together a lot of experience and given himself a conviction."

"Exactly, Doctor." He busied himself with a beer for a guy who'd come in. When he came back he stood for a moment, smiling, then he said, diffidently:

"You have such a hunch, Dr. Connor?"

"I think I have, Julius. And it's not about a horse."

"No?" He turned to ring up money on the register and reached for the bar rag. Jack was busy at the other end. I felt as though something important were happening to me. I said no, it wasn't about a horse, it was about a woman. Julius continued wiping the bar. He spoke directly to the mahogany:

"In that case, I should say by all means to play your hunch."

"Why?"

"If your hunch is correct, you will be very pleased, will you not?"

"Of course."

". . . and if it is not correct, you will have gained, shall I say, wisdom?"

I paid my bill and walked back down Seventh Avenue wondering just what sort of wisdom I was going to gain if my hunch misfired. But I also knew that I was going to start on the Panty Burke business all over again, basing every move I made on the exact statements of Grace Larkin. She had to be completely right or completely wrong. The very nature of all the evidence proved that.

I hadn't been able to rid myself of the hunch that she had been telling the truth. If so, and if Burke had been the sort of a heel her story would have made him, his call to her the night he'd killed Peters wasn't one of affection.

I wondered, dimly, if Grace Larkin's beautiful body would be the next one to be found someplace.

Of the people in the case—the five we knew were directly involved—two were dead, one was a murderer at large, one was gone from her apartment and probably in imminent danger, and the only other one was in Boston, apparently minding her own business.

There wasn't anything I could do to help the police catch Burke or to find Grace Larkin . . .

I caught the "Merchants" to Boston. I'd called Katie and got a lot of admonition, located Stirnie Maize and, after some fooling around, learned the place Midge Manson lived. The guy who'd lent her the money had it.

I dug my way out of the crowd in the Back Bay station and walked over to the Copley Plaza. The bellboy took my bags up and I grabbed a cab and headed for Wickland Street. We rode a long time in all directions, as you do in Boston, and finally came to the neighborhood. The driver had to peer out at street signs. It was pretty broken down.

Wickland was a short, dirty alley full of wall-to-wall brick tenements. We sorted out number 37 and I paid off the hack. There was a light in the hallway and some mail boxes. Sure enough, Mrs. Midge Manson was on one of them. There was only one bell and I pushed that. Nothing happened. I lit a cigarette and waited. Then I pushed the bell again. After a while I heard some footsteps thumping inside and a monstrous fat woman came to the door. She said:

"Well?"

"I want to see Mrs. Manson. Is she in?"

"I guess so." She bellied her way back into the hall and yelled upstairs. "Midge . . ."

"Yeah?"

"Man here to see you. Want him up there?"

"Wait a minute." There was some moving around up above and a pair of slippered feet appeared at the top of the stairs. "What do you want, Mister?"

"Grace Larkin asked me to talk to you. I'm from New York."

"The hell she did! What about?"

"She's in some kind of trouble and she thought . . ."

"Okay, Mister, come up."

The fat woman sluffed her way to the back of the house and I climbed the stairs. Midge Manson was waiting at her door and said for me to come in. The place was like any other tenement and it smelled. She'd evidently made some effort to keep it neat because the curtains were clean and there wasn't much junk around. She was baby-faced cute. Around thirty. I sat in the good chair, by invitation, and she sat on the edge of the bed.

"You a cop?"

"No."

"What are you then?"

"I'm a doctor. A friend of Grace's."

"Yeah?"

"Yeah. My name is Connor . . ."

"Oh."

"You know me?"

"Sure. I heard about you." She went over to a cupboard by the electric plate. "Want a drink, Doc?"

"No, thanks. I had dinner on the train coming up. Help yourself, though." She did. But plenty. She came back and sat down. She had on some kind of a bathrobe and was careless about it. She said, "Now what?"

"Well, I'll tell you, Midge, I know Grace pretty well and she's told me a lot about what went on a few months ago—between your late husband, Panty Burke and Peters—and now she's disappeared. You've read the papers?"

"Yeah. I've read the papers."

"You know how it is, then. The way it looks is that Burke turned out to be a first-class heel . . ."

"You ain't just kidding, Mister!"

". . . looks like he'd given Grace the brush-off, had never gone to Florida at all, then turned up in New York to kill Peters."

She blinked a little. "That's right. Then what?"

"Then, after he's killed Peters, he calls Grace Larkin up and asks her to join him, to run off with him."

"That isn't true . . ." It came out so fast it even startled her.

"Why?"

She buried her nose in her drink. When she'd gulped down some of the liquor she said, "You just said he was a heel, didn't you? After he'd ditched her once, why would he go back after her?"

I said, "Do you want to tell me how all this happened?"

"Why should I? It's all been in the papers. Burke took up with a bad guy, threw us out because we didn't dare fight him back and stole every cent we had. Ain't that enough?"

"Not quite, Midge." She looked up at my tone and I felt her stiffen. "There were some other things that need explaining," She was clearly frightened, as though she knew what I was about to say.

"What things?"

"How well did Pike know Grace Larkin?"

She threw back her head and laughed. Relieved.

"What the hell are you getting at? He didn't know her at all."

"You sure?"

"Of course. We saw the woman once, one night at a club. That was when Burke and Pike were arguing about their business. I had to sit and talk to her. She's a crow. That's the only time Pike ever spoke to the dame."

"That's what you think!" I said it just that way, too. Hard.

She climbed off the bed stiff-legged and stood in front of my chair. Her face, was tight and her teeth bared. For a second I thought I'd better get up, too.

"What was that you said?" She put every word carefully into my face. It was very nasty.

"I said that maybe that's what you thought."

"I think you'd better explain that crack." She didn't budge, just kept burning that vicious stare into me.

"All right, I will. I don't know whether you know anything about it or not. I don't even know whether it makes any difference or not. But I do know that Pike Manson was on intimate terms with Grace."

"That's a lie." She didn't need any show of temper to make it very unpleasant. She just said it. Then, very deliberately, she said it again. "That's a lie."

"Maybe it is, Midge. Maybe there's something I don't understand about the facts. Facts, you know, are pretty hard to deny just by hollering that something's a lie."

"What facts?" Those baby blue eyes looked like glistening quartz.

"For one, the fact that Pike left his razor in her bathroom."

"What?" This time she did yell. She started to shake. She gave me a double take and said, "Wait a minute." She marched to the cupboard again and poured herself another drink. She drank this one straight down, shivered again, headed for the sink as though she was about to lose it, and finally walked slowly back and dropped down on the bed.

"Tell me that again."

"Pike Manson left his razor in Grace Larkin's bathroom; she had it hidden in her medicine cabinet. From the way it had been put away, I judged that she had been running around with Manson about the time she had been on friendly terms with Burke as well."

"His razor! What makes you think it was Pike's razor?"

"What kind of a razor did he use?"

"An electric razor. A Schick. He'd been using them since they first came out."

". . . he never used any other kind?"

"No." She seemed almost eager, no hardness now, just relief, or grabbing at a straw. "He used to talk about electric shavers with every man he met. From the time they came out he never used any other kind."

"That makes it a little complicated."

"Why?"

"Because this wasn't an electric razor. It was a very unusual razor. Pike may never have shaved with it, I don't know. I've no proof that he had."

"Then what . . ."

"You see, Midge, I *do* have proof, at least, that he handled it."

"Handled it."

"Yes. Definite proof. His fingerprints were on it."

There was a long silence. The ball was in her court and I wasn't willing to break the spell. She would have something to say. I don't know how fond she had been of Manson, nor do I know how fond she might have been of Burke. I do know she had shown a bitter, spitting jealousy when I accused Manson of two-timing her. Now she just sat there. It was definitely my turn to wait her out. After a while she looked up again.

"Pike's fingerprints, eh?"

"Yes. Checked with Washington."

"I see." She let down, deflated. She looked small and tired. "Okay, Doc. Maybe it was that way. You can't ever tell, can you?"

I said you couldn't and studied the change in her manner. She looked around as though she were looking for a way to get out.

"Look, Doc, if Pike knew the Larkin woman that well I didn't know anything about it. She tell you that?"

"No. I found the razor."

"Do the cops know about it?"

"Yes. I showed them the prints."

"I see."

"Does that make any difference in the story, Midge? Does that fact make it any easier for you to talk?"

"What do you mean, talk?"

"Isn't there anything that you can add to the story? About Ernie Peters, maybe?"

"Why, no. There's nothing to add. So Burke was a heel, in his way, and maybe Pike was a heel in his. What difference does that make? I'm the only one it affects."

I had to admit that was true. She didn't offer to cry or anything, just sat there and drank more whisky. Got more careless with the bathrobe. Finally, I said:

"Tell me about Pike's death."

"He boozed himself to death. It was all in the papers."

"I mean tell me about why—surely he had a lot to say during those drunken spells . . ."

"I don't see why."

"Listen, kid. You seem like a right little guy to me. The people that put you in this spot are running loose. You've got every right to want to see them pay for it. If there's the smallest fact you can add about Peters, or Burke, or even Pike, you should say so."

"What the hell's the use, Doc. What can I gain except to get myself killed? If I read the papers right, the cops are after both Panty and the Larkin woman. What can I add to that? You know how I hated them both." She ran her hand through her bright hair. "At least you ought to know if you've followed this thing."

"What makes you think you'd get yourself killed?"

"Peters got himself killed."

"Peters was badly involved. Are you?"

"You didn't see any cops outside, did you?" She looked at her fingernails and climbed off the bed. "They were out there. There were out there for weeks." She walked unsteadily to the bureau and got an orange stick and came back to the bed. "They asked me all the questions in the world." She dug at her nails.

"They asked me all the questions in the world, Doc. Then they went away."

"Yeah?"

"Yeah!" She grinned, a bit punchy. "So you ask me questions, and so you can go away, now, too."

I tried to get another rise out of her on the subject of Pike Manson's infidelity. "How do you suppose Pike got tangled up with Grace Larkin, Midge?"

No rise. Never after that first time. "I don't know. I don't know if he was tangled up with her and I don't know why he would have been. Is that good enough?"

"It'll have to be."

"That's right. It'll have to be." She chucked the orange stick on the bed. "Now do you go?"

"Yes. Now I go." I picked up my hat and coat. I still couldn't figure out why she had suddenly become so calm over Pike's relationship with Grace. "Aren't you pretty sore about finding out that Pike was hanging around the Larkin girl?"

She looked at me with her distorted, drunken face and laughed. "Know what, Doc?"

"What?"

"That's a question which could be of interest only to another hippopotamus."

She laughed again while I was picking up my coat and hat. Loud. Loud and hysterically. As I climbed down the dark stairway, she was still laughing. I heard the crash of a glass against a wall up there. Then she stopped laughing.

As I went through the hallway to the door, I saw the fat woman watching me leave.

9

I took a noonish train home Sunday, not quite sure what I'd accomplished. At least I'd added an impression of another of the five who had started out together to make the Panty Burke story.

Midge Manson didn't belong in the same league with Grace Larkin, but she was tough. Intelligent, too, I think. A mean little woman with savvy and guts enough to take care of herself. I am certain that the news of Pike's philandering was a shock to her. I am equally certain that, once she'd believed it, she locked up for the night. I can't forget her blazing indignation, then her hard acceptance, with laughter.

Pike's razor. Midge had come out with the electric razor information without fencing about it. It could have been anybody's razor at that. Actually, all we knew was that Manson's prints were on it. Maybe he just used it one morning. It could have been Burke's. It still didn't make Grace look too good.

There I go again, using Eddie Marsh's case instead of the one I had decided to work out for myself. Grace Larkin, in my case, *had* to look good. Ergo: no Manson visit-and-shave. Budge says the fiend. Budge not says Gobbo.

I couldn't put Midge and Burke together, could I? Eddie Marsh hadn't, after a hell of a lot of digging. I couldn't on account of trying to believe Burke hadn't been a heel about the thing.

It was still miserable in New York and I trudged my way to a cab and on home. The living room smelled like fireplace

and I inspected. There were live coals and a smoldering piece
of my dollar wood. The Christmas tree had packages under it.
I looked at one of the tags. It said, "To Doc darling, with love
from Katie."

I looked on the desk for a note and there was one. "I have
cleaned out your refrigerator and defrosted it. The thing was
a disgrace. Also, there is a custom among civilized Americans
to mend socks that have holes in them instead of shoving them
aside and buying new ones. I have taken an immense group of
them home. Call me when you get back. Love, Katie."

I called her. The conversation was private. Most of it, at
any rate. She did say that Eddie Marsh had called while she was
playing house and left word for me to call him when I came in.
She didn't tell him I'd been in Boston. I rang Eddie at his place.

"Where you been?" He sounded happy enough.

I stalled. "Katie told me you'd called while I was out."

It worked. He went on from there. "Yeah. I dropped in to
tell you a couple of things . . . and maybe ask you a question."

"Good. Tell and ask."

"Okay. You sound fresh as paint. You been drinking?"

"I've been talking to Katie."

"That would account for it." He made a fast shift to serious.
"Doc. Listen. I want to come over for a few minutes. Is Katie
there?"

"Of course not."

"Well I didn't know and . . ."

I told him to come on over and spent a few minutes thinking about people catching Katie sorting socks at my apartment.
Virtuous people like Eddie get ideas. I made up my mind to get
that key back immediately after Christmas. And yet it had been
kind of wonderful to come home and find her tracks. Dammit,
I still say it's people's best qualities that get them into the most
trouble. In this world of devious thinking the worst thing you
can do is to be forthright.

I was thinking about that sort of thing when Eddie pounded
up. I herded him in. Getting Eddie into any place and at rest is
a little like a switchyard problem. He's too big for everything

and has to be maneuvered. I backed him into the big chair and went after a drink, wondering what he had on his mind. When I came back, I got it.

"Doc. I take it for granted that you know we would keep a fair kind of an eye on Midge Manson."

Ain't it wonderful? I must learn humility, sometime. It lets you take for granted the fact that other people may be smart, too. The Old Doc used to say so. I should have learned that, when Eddie puts up his dough, he has 'em back to back. I said something inappropriate and waited.

"I think you should have let me know before you went to Boston."

"Maybe I should have." I started to act mysterious and decided against it. There isn't a lot of private life you can have, once the Department gets interested in you. "As a matter of fact, Eddie, I didn't get anything up there."

"Will you tell me about it?"

"Of course. I just went on a hunch."

"What sort of a hunch?"

"Well . . ." What do you say to a factual guy like this? "I went on the hunch that Grace Larkin was telling the truth."

"Great! When? And about what?"

"That Panty Burke had *really* intended to meet her in Florida. That she had had no criminal knowledge of the counterfeiting. That she had had no . . . really complicating relations with Manson."

"You thought that, did you?"

"I figured it might be possible."

"Do you know what *might* be possible, Doc?"

"What?"

"It *might* be possible that you have made yourself responsible for some sort of an attempt on Midge Manson."

He let me think about it. I said, "It doesn't fit, Eddie. Why would there be an attack on Midge?"

"Because I think she's the only person left of the five of them who can give us the answers. I don't think she knows it . . . and we can't beat it out of her. I think she's in danger, Doc." He fussed with his drink. "That's why we still have men on her. We think Burke may try to kill her for what she knows."

"She said there were no more cops."

"That's swell. We wanted her to say that." Eddie grunted comfortably and settled back with his drink. "There are cops."

"So I judge."

"How about telling me about it?"

I told him, exactly as it happened. Eddie listened carefully and made a couple of notes in his little black book. We went over the razor business with a lot of care. After a while he said:

"Your trip to Boston may blow the whole thing wide open. I can't afford to take a chance on your blundering into any more solutions. You're just stupid enough to add up all the wrong figures and come up with the right answer. If you get what I mean."

"I get it." I had him off balance for once and followed it up. "You think maybe I'm right—that Larkin and Panty Burke are nice people after all."

"I don't think anything of the kind! They're bums! All of them! Panty Burke is a proved murderer. Midge Manson, I'm convinced, knows the facts that would convict him, even if we didn't have the physical evidence. So you have to go to Boston and advertise the news that you've turned amateur detective! Great!" Eddie sulked in his huge way and finished his drink. "The feeling between Burke and Midge Manson is really bad. I'm convinced she could convict him, whether she knows it or not. Also, I'm convinced she wants to. Sooner or later either she *will* convict Burke or we'll find her body someplace. I should have added that I believe Burke doesn't care to be convicted."

"That makes it very plain." I couldn't help adding, "If it's true."

He said, "What makes you think it isn't true?"

I had to say, "Damned if I know, Eddie. Maybe it's just a hunch. There's something wrong about the whole thing. When I find out I'll be able to answer a lot more of your questions."

"When you find out, Panty Burke will kill you—and I doubt if we'll be able to prevent it—unless you want a cordon around the joint."

"That would be better than getting killed, wouldn't it?"

"I was thinking about the poor cops who would have to keep track of you. On the whole, I think it's to the best interests of everybody concerned to let you get killed. We'd probably get Burke shortly after he did it."

"You have swell ideas. So now I'm murdered in my bed."

"I think you're pretty safe, frankly. I'm just calling to your attention the fact that, if your strange hunch should be right, and anybody concerned finds out about it, you're the target. See?"

"I wouldn't like it. I didn't care for Ernie Peters' appearance last time I saw him." Eddie put his black notebook back in his pocket and frowned at me.

"You better think about it, Doc. This fella's not going to hesitate over killing the next guy that gets in his way. Frankly I can't see how you could do him any damage. He can read the papers and he knows we've got him dead to rights—prints, everything. But . . ."

"But what?"

"There may be some angle about Larkin or Midge Manson that you'd get tangled up in that'd make it bad for you. Why don't you leave it alone?"

"I'm curious, I guess. I've got a hunch about everybody in the case, and none of my hunches fits with your evidence." I watched the big guy get restless in his chair. But he didn't have anything to say. "I have a hunch, for instance, that Grace Larkin is all right, that she's as much puzzled by Burke's actions as anybody."

Eddie said, "Rats!"

"I've also got a hunch that Midge Manson is nasty, altogether bad, and that she's as smart as a weasel. That she's up to here in it someway."

"What's your hunch on Peters?" Eddie seemed almost interested.

"I think Peters was much further in, someway, than it looks."

"Why do you think that?"

"He was too scared. If it had only been mutuel tickets, he'd have already adjusted his thinking to the risk. It was worse than that."

"It could be that way." Marsh leaned back and stared at the ceiling. "Peters knew too much about Burke. That's sure. Now what's your hunch on Burke, himself?"

"I think Burke tried to go to Florida . . ."

"Yeah?"

"Yeah. Something, or somebody, stopped him. What's more, I think he had pretty well cleared out of whatever he'd been in with Peters, or Pike Manson, or whoever it was."

"Couldn't be. Not in light of what's happened." Eddie shook his head. "The guy was in deep, even if you give him credit for trying to get straightened out."

"My hunch won't let it be that way. You go ahead and catch Burke and convict him. That's the way it probably is. I'm just going to have some fun believing *everything* Grace Larkin told me."

"You poor sap! That would have you believing that Burke didn't even kill Peters!"

"I won't go that far, of course, but I'll bet it wasn't because Burke was criminally involved."

"Oh mister! You're nuts!" Eddie patted his breast pocket. "I've got enough stuff right here in my book to blow up all your hunches."

"I suppose you have." At that I guess I was half kidding. I certainly didn't have much to go on. "All the same, Eddie, don't be surprised if you end up arresting some guy named Maximilian Wardhouse."

"Okay, okay." Eddie loomed up to his feet. "But, in the meantime, if Maximilian Wardhouse killed Ernie Peters and you find out about it, you better have a bulletproof vest."

"I'll watch out." I helped him with his coat. "But keep an eye peeled for Maximilian."

Eddie grinned. "So now I got to start being a teletype jockey again. That, I refuse to do. You'll have to look for this Wardhouse by yourself. I got enough trouble as it is. Be seeing you, kid."

I sat there a while and listened to the elevator complaining its way down with the big guy.

It could be Maximilian Wardhouse, at that.

10

I met Katie after her show on Tuesday and we set off for Beekman Place to gather up the turkey and stuff. The queen-of-love-and-beauty was really leaping. She'd apparently been busier than a pup with a rubber ball because when we got to the Beekman Place apartment, there were pots and pans and packages all over the place.

Katie said, "It'll probably take two cabs."

It did. It took exactly four trips down in the elevator, two because of the necessity for not spilling things and two more because of things we forgot. The doorman helped some but got in the way a lot. For a while it was like a Ladies' Aid Supper—everybody running around with armloads of stuff and asking questions.

In my own, less busy elevator, it was simpler. We just loaded everything in and out while it waited. In something less than an hour we had settled down in front of the fire. The tree lights were on and I'd opened a bottle of champagne. It was all very gay.

I said, "Merry Christmas," and we tossed off a drink. Then Katie said, "Merry Christmas," and we tossed off another. After that had gone on for a while, I brought Katie up to date on my Boston trip. I told her about Eddie's visit, too. She thought all this over quite somberly.

"That's like you."

I asked her what was and she said, "To introduce Maximilian Wardhouse into the picture."

"Well, it's got to be somebody hypothetical if it's not Burke."

"Very sound, Doctor, very sound." We had a toast to the soundness of Maximilian as an hypothesis. Then we drank one to Maximilian, himself. This, however, Katie felt was unjustified.

"It should have been a hypothetical drink, not a real one. As it is now, we're a drink ahead of our toasts."

"What do you propose?"

"I propose Merry Christmas." Katie is nothing if not practical. "That will catch us up nicely and we can go on from there."

I agreed that this, also, was very sound.

About four-thirty, Bobby, the janitor's boy, knocked on the office door and announced that he had something in his eye. It looked pretty badly irritated, with reason. Katie found a substantial hunk of coal in it. Katie is wonderful at taking things out of people's eyes. She has less feeling than I, too, about mixing champagne and first aid.

The postman brought a handful of Christmas cards and some casual mail which I chucked on the desk. One of the envelopes caught my eye because it was bulky, looked as though it might have something solid in it. I tore it open.

Wrapped in a piece of paper was a key. It was the key to a self-checking compartment. Number 284. That's all. No letter, nothing. I showed it to Katie and we started guessing. Somebody wanted me to find something, that was sure. Then, too, it had to be somebody who couldn't, or, at least, didn't want to, turn up in person.

Because it was pretty obvious the key was connected with the Burke business, it would be one of the people connected with it. Would Burke, himself, want to send me anything?

Katie had opinions on the subject. "Why would Burke send you anything? It would be more likely somebody like Grace Larkin or the babe you got drunk with in Boston."

"I believe you're jealous."

"Of course I am. What am I to expect with you running around all over the country chasing these dames?"

"I'm not chasing dames. I'm chasing a killer . . . a guy."

"What makes you think it's a guy?"

I had to admit that I didn't know what made me think it was a guy. If Eddie Marsh's evidence wasn't right, it could have been anybody. Even Maximilian Wardhouse. Then Katie made a point:

"How long do they leave the stuff in those lockers if you don't claim it?"

"I haven't any idea . . . What? Twenty-four hours."

"Well, what are we waiting for, then? Whoever sent the key probably knew how long they'd leave the contents of the locker. You're supposed to go right after it."

I said where did we look and she said we should try Grand Central. We had some more champagne and set off. When we got to Grand Central, it wasn't much of a trick to locate the bank of boxes which included the two hundreds and there was our prize, a carefully wrapped package with my name and address neatly printed in ink. Katie was eaten up by curiosity and was all for sitting on the stairway to the lower level while we opened it up.

"Does it tick?" We listened and it didn't tick. I said, "Come on. Let's go home."

Katie sniffed. "Home?"

"Want to make something of it?"

"Not especially." We breezed out into Vanderbilt Avenue. "Home," remarked my little friend, "is where the champagne is."

I looked around for a cab. There were hundreds of them, as always, but other people with packages were piling into them and riding away. Katie looked flushed and beautiful as she trotted across the street after me. "They are seldom today, aren't they!"

"What are seldom?"

"Empty cabs."

I saw a high flag and grabbed a door handle. I said, "What do you want? Two? Get in."

Katie said, "Merry Christmas," and I said it right back at her. That was so we'd be two toasts ahead of our drinking when we got back. At the door, the cab driver said Merry Christmas, too, so we were four drinks ahead when we'd exchanged greetings all around.

The fire felt good and we sat down to open the first Christmas package, Merry Christmas to Doc from Grand Central Station.

I cut the string, carefully preserving the knot, I don't know why, and unwrapped the box. I knew that, sooner or later, I'd have to explain the thing to Eddie Marsh and I wanted to do it right.

The brown manila paper had been used before, the sort of stuff you find around any house. The printed address matched the scrawl on the envelope which had held the key.

The box had come from a grocery store, probably, because it was of the corrugated material manufacturers use to ship canned foods. It had been neatly cut down and what printing remained indicated it had originally contained somebody's evaporated milk.

Inside was an assortment of smaller packages and, at the bottom several tin things which Katie recognized as cookie cutters. They were shaped as squares, diamonds and rectangles. Among the flat packages was a note addressed simply to Doc.

> Dear Doc,
> Thank you for all your help. I'm asking one more favor, if you're still willing to string along. These things are Panty's. They've been checked and a friend got them for me. Will you keep them for a while? You may look at anything here, although I doubt if any of it would be of value to you or to the police. I think the police must have searched my place already because Panty's English razor is missing. I am staying out of circulation until the man who shot Ernie Peters is caught.
> Sincerely,
>
> Grace Larkin.

Katie said, "Flordoeuvre." She was examining the metal things.

"That's it. These were the cutters Burke had used to experiment with shapes and sizes." I put them out on the couch. "He's got a diamond one—you'd think he'd have had a spade and a heart and a club."

"That goes to show he knew more about the sandwich business than you do."

"Why?"

Katie picked up the diamond one. "If he'd been making his hors d'oeuvre out of dough, he could have used any shape without wasting material. He'd just roll out the scraps again and cut them up. But he planned to use slices of bread so he had to use regular shapes like squares and diamonds. See?"

"Yeah. That wouldn't occur to a guy who was just stalling with a phony idea, would it!"

"I wouldn't think so." Katie got up and started for the kitchen. "It's pretty sordid, isn't it! The whole thing annoys me. I'm getting dinner." She went on into the kitchen and rattled a pan. I followed her out.

"What do you mean, sordid? It's kind of pathetic, I think."

"Of course it's pathetic!" She dropped an emphatic pan. "It's pathetic when you read that the condemned man ate a hearty breakfast, too, but there's nothing very wholesome about it."

"No. There isn't much about any of the story that's what you'd call wholesome."

"What's more, it's very damned unChristmas Evey. Go put that stuff away and get out your guitar."

"It got two broken strings. I haven't touched it for months."

"Well, I have. And it hasn't got any broken strings. It has six beautiful new Nylon strings and they're in tune, or were Sunday."

Oh Katie, Katie, Katie!

I piled Burke's stuff back into the box and put it in the office—and forgot it. The ash trays needed emptying and I pulled out the table from the wall. Under shouted and expert instruction from the kitchen, I found small glass holders and red candles. I asked if we were to have a tablecloth.

"We are. A very beautiful one from my hope chest."

"I didn't know girls had hope chests any more."

"I could say quite a lot about that, my friend. Here's the tablecloth. You'll have to fold it or it'll drag."

"How long have you had a hope chest?"

"Too long, you lug. I'm thinking of using it for a window-box. Look out . . ."

The roaster lid hit the floor at my feet, exposing a most wonderful turkey, one of the eight-pounders that make you wish you had never heard of a big one. I hustled out to set the table and, from there on, Katie took over. It was Christmas magic.

It was candlelighted magic, with talk about childhood and almost forgotten things like Katie's old dog and my pony. The champagne stood in our glasses, almost untouched.

Between courses—and there were courses which Katie bore, flushed and triumphant from the little kitchen—between courses we opened our packages. The Jensen serving dish was a shining success and, of all things, I found a rather wonderful medium-weight topcoat hanging in the closet. A beautiful scarf under the tree had contained a clue. There were other things, silly and happymaking, the thoughtful dime-store jokes that take more time and love than even coats and platters.

After dinner we washed the dishes together and packed Katie's things into the roaster and the empty pots. The candles we put on the mantel. I poked around with the fire as Katie finished the last of the chores and powdered her nose. She turned from the mirror:

"Now how about the guitar?"

I got the old box out and, sure enough, there were fine, new strings, almost in tune—new Nylon strings which are just like gut and can be played as a guitar should be played, with the fingers.

We sang . . . and sang. All the old, familiar carols and some ancient ballad favorites of the Old Doc's generation—*Dear Old Girl* and *I Had a Dream, Dear*, I sang lead and Katie harmonized with a sweet, sure alto that never missed.

When the fire had burned low there were church bells outside and Katie looked at her watch. She walked to the window and looked out. It was snowing gently. The chimes were playing *Adeste Fidelis*, but I always think of it as *Oh Come All Ye Faithful*.

Katie said, "Oh Come All Ye Faithful."

I said, "Yeah."

She stood with her back to the window. "Get your hat, Jimmy."

11

I had my key in the latch when I heard the phone ringing. It would be Katie with a last good night and a final Merry Christmas. It was Grace Larkin.

"Doc?" Her voice was muffled and cautious. "I can't talk long. I'm afraid I'm being watched."

"Okay, Grace, I won't ask questions."

"Did you get the package from Grand Central?"

"Yes. This afternoon."

"Good. The room where I'm . . . living was searched the other night and I don't know what they were after so I sent you everything I had of Panty's. It wasn't here. It was stored, but the check was here."

"Are you in danger?"

"I think so, Doc, and I can't figure out why. I suppose you've guessed why I left my apartment so suddenly."

"No." Then, "The telephone call, of course."

"Yes. It was a woman. I didn't know the voice. She said she had just *seen* Panty Burke kill a man and that he wouldn't stand a chance to get away if the police ever got hold of me, that Panty had said for me to get out and stay out, that if I didn't, she was going to take care of me, personally."

"No wonder you were so frightened!"

"I wasn't frightened. I was sunk. I'd had the idea that Panty had been killed. Then to find out he was alive and had killed someone! I hadn't quite believed you when you told me, or it hadn't penetrated, somehow. The idea that this woman had actually seen him kill a man was . . . sickening."

"Why are you calling me now . . . anything more than to find out about the package?"

"Yes. I think I need your advice, if not your help. If, of course, you're still willing to give it . . ."

"More than ever, Grace. There's something completely fishy about the Peters killing and I'm curious. Tell me."

"I have a wonderfully loyal friend in town, a little dress-maker who's done some sewing for me. When I left my apartment, I came to her in the night and she took me in. I am quite certain that nobody in New York, or anyplace, knows I would have gone to her. I'm also quite certain I wasn't followed here, yet someone has found me and searched my room. It couldn't have been the police. They'd have taken me in for questioning, wouldn't they?"

"Yes. They would have. As a matter of fact, I think you should go to the police with your story. Is that why you want my advice?"

"In a way, yes. I'm absolutely certain, now, that Panty Burke is being made use of in some way—framed or something of that sort."

"Why do you think so?"

"Because there must be some new people mixed up in it. . . . After all, with Peters dead, Panty is the only man left who was in any way involved with the old trouble, and if Panty had killed Peters by accident or any other way, he wouldn't have some woman call me up and threaten me. The only other woman concerned that I know of is Midge Manson and she wouldn't help him if he were dying."

"So you think that the people who are bothering you are not connected with the original trouble?"

"How could they be? If it isn't Panty it's got to be somebody new. Will you think about it that way, Doc?"

"I've been thinking about it that way. It doesn't make any sense. The police's case does make sense."

"That's why I can't give myself up yet—that and the fact that, if I am being watched, I'll find out who it is if it's the last thing I ever do."

"It might be, you know, at that."

"I know. I'll be careful. May I call you again?"

"Whenever you like. What about the advice?"

"Thanks, Doc. I don't think I really wanted advice. I was scared and wanted bracing up." She laughed a little. "So long."

I was still hollering wait a minute when she hung up.

There didn't seem to be anything to do but go to bed, so I turned off the tree lights and started to undress. The feeling that Grace Larkin might be seriously threatened stuck with me. I should have made her tell me where she was. Or I should have sold her on going to Eddie Marsh. If it were, as she said, new people and not Burke, she had nothing to lose. As it was, she had plenty to lose.

I decided to call Eddie. He's a bachelor and has a phone in his bedroom. The phone rang exactly once.

"Marsh!" You'd think he'd just been called out of a conference.

I said Merry Christmas. He said things about is this a gag and you're drunk. He didn't sound too mad, though, and finally came out with a Merry Christmas and where had I been?

"I went to Midnight Mass with Katie."

"I did too, without Katie, worse luck. What's on your mind?"

"I've just talked to Grace Larkin."

"The hell you have! Is she there?"

"No. I wish she was . . ." I told him the whole story and he listened carefully, making me repeat parts of it. Finally:

"Can you sleep late in the morning?"

"Sure. Why, Eddie?"

"This damned thing gets me nuts. I've got some stuff here that may make sense with what you just told me. I'd like to come over."

"How about cold turkey and champagne?"

"Are you kidding?"

"All here for you. Come on."

"Wonderful. Doc. Larkin said 'dressmaker' . . . just like that?"

"Yes. I think she said 'little dressmaker'—you know that always means little in the sense of not very successful."

"Okay, Doc, I'll call the Department and be right over."

I looked into my now spotless refrigerator and hauled out the cold turkey and a bottle of champagne which I set out on the living-room table. My watch said two forty-five. A quick shower made it three o'clock and Eddie was at the door. I put on a bathrobe and let him in.

"Where's that turkey?"

"What's the matter? Didn't you have dinner?"

"No. I worked. Apparently you did have dinner."

"But the best. My beautiful Katie fixed it. Sit down."

Eddie started to sit down on my guitar and I had presence of mind to goose him. He almost broke the mantel down, but it saved the guitar. Eddie's got a little weakness that way and is sometimes persecuted by his friends. He looked at the instrument.

"Geetar, eh? You ought to play it oftener. I don't see enough of your sweeter side." He found a place to sit down. "You sing, too?"

"Like a bird. Have some turkey and a mug of bubbly. I want to talk about Grace Larkin."

"So do I." There was a drumstick left and I gave him that. He went after it like a small boy. Through a healthy mouthful, he said, "Grace Larkin has been acting all wrong."

"How?"

"Several ways. She shouldn't have called you up, for one thing."

"Without going into the reasons why I think she *should* have called me, why do you think she shouldn't have?"

"Because if she knows the things I think she does about Peters' killing, she has no business calling anybody up. That's one of the reasons." I poured him a glass of champagne.

"What are the others?"

"If she knows where Burke is, she's nuts to tell anybody she's staying with her old dressmaker. We'll have her before tomorrow night if she stays there."

"I agree."

"Then, what's all this about her being observed . . . and the guff about her room being searched? If Burke is taking chances like that, we'd have had him long ago. If she's telling the truth, it isn't Burke."

"That's what I think."

"What? That she's telling the truth?"

"That she's telling the truth *and* that she's being observed *and* that her room was searched *and* that Burke isn't anywhere around."

"Who could it be? There isn't anybody left for it to be."

"Midge?"

"Why Midge?"

"I'm damned if I know. She hates Burke."

"When was the room searched?"

"Grace said a couple of days ago."

"Midge Mansori hasn't left her usual haunts since . . . in a long time." Eddie looked at the bare drumstick a little wistfully. I found a thigh for him. "You saw her Saturday night."

"You say she hasn't been away from her haunts since . . . since when?" The big cop glowered at the turkey. "You holding out on me, Eddie?"

"A little. I told you I had some stuff to exchange."

"Has Midge been in New York?"

"Yes."

"When?"

"Okay, Doc, you can have it for what it's worth. I can't make it fit any place. She was here the afternoon Peters was killed. She came here on a morning train and left that evening."

"Know where she went in New York?"

"No. Not until afterward. When Boston learned she'd gone they let us know and we went up there afterward and talked to her. Her story was straight enough and the fact that she'd let everybody know she was going didn't leave me enough to hold her on. She hasn't budged since."

"What did she say she did in New York?"

"Some very ordinary things like shopping. She had receipts. She went to the loan-shark where she'd hocked her ring and got it back. Had her savings book with her, including the withdrawal she used. She'd got it the hard way. A few bucks at a time."

"Where was she when Peters was shot?" I'd neglected to tell Eddie that Larkin had quoted the telephone woman as saying she saw Panty kill Peters. I decided to keep on neglecting it for a while.

"I don't know, frankly. She wasn't seen around there."

"Neither was Panty Burke. Where'd she say she was?"

"Having something to eat at the station. Nobody remembers her."

"She's a bad gal."

"I have no doubt of it. A problem for the Boston Morals Squad." Eddie chucked the thigh bone into the fire and said "Sorry." He looked very well fed and comfortable. He lit a cigarette and gave me the big grin. "Now you want to hear some stuff?"

"Very much. Shoot."

"Well, Doc, in return for your being a very nice young fella and keeping your nose clean with the Department, I am permitted to give you certain information which otherwise . . ."

I said, "I can wait."

". . . which, otherwise, would have been withheld. Your much abused friend, Panty Burke, has been leaving tracks."

"Recent ones, you mean?"

"As recent as last Saturday. How do you like them apples?"

"Give!"

"I'll tell you, chum, I'd undoubtedly give sooner or later without further champagne, but since my habit of abstinence extends only through my . . ."

"Please! Here's champagne. Here's lots of it. I not only want to hear the news but that droning kills me. Save it for running for office or something." For a big, silent cop, the guy, on occasion, spouts words like a hose spouts water. "Tell me stuff!"

"On Saturday afternoon at four forty-five, the Police Department was advised that someone had broken into a little used warehouse of the"—Eddie consulted his black book—"Landroff Grocery Company in Harlem and removed, therefrom, a considerable quantity of foodstuffs."

"So?"

"So we investigated. As a matter of fact, we investigated very thoroughly as is our custom even in apparently routine robberies of this sort . . ."

"Okay, public-relations, the Department is wonderful. Now, how did it get to the great Marsh of Homicide?"

"It seems that some kids around there had seen a guy drive up in a truck, open the door without unnecessary fuss and haul out a lot of cases of stuff and drive away. The warehouse is seldom used and the kids took it for granted it was okay."

"Out of the way place?"

"Very. Down near the water. All warehouses and old storage places. There's a lumber yard there." Eddie sipped his champagne, smacked his lips, took a big pull. "Wonderful stuff. It goes up your nose."

"Some kids saw the man."

"That's right. They didn't pay much attention to him, as I say, but they *did* notice that it was a rented truck. A drive-yourself job. Of course we went to work on it and finally found it. The vehicle had been rented from a small operator who has only two trucks. A man had seen his sign and come in at about three o'clock showing a driver's license in the name of"—the black book again—"Phillip Sewell Baker. He'd signed a form with that name, deposited fifty dollars and drove off with his truck. An hour later he was back, paid the minimum rental and left."

"Who is Phillip Sewell Baker?"

"Phillip Sewell Baker is a gent whose intemperate habits led him to lie down for a while, last week, in Central. Park. While he was resting somebody pinched his poke." I poured more champagne for both of us at this picture of degradation. Eddie went on. "For reasons of his own, Mr. Baker had not reported this incident."

"A weak character."

"Undoubtedly. But here's the pretty part. We went over the truck for anything we could find. The fellow had worn gloves and there were no fingerprints. But there was a footprint, a beauty. It was perfectly patterned on a fairly clean piece of wrapping paper."

"Where was it?"

"All nicely sheltered in the body of the truck, impressed deeply because he was probably carrying a box of heavy stuff at the time."

"And you had Burke's prints?"

"A perfect one from the room where he killed Peters. These were the same, the same shoes, anyway."

"What had he stolen? He must be planning to hole in."

"You aren't kidding." The book again. "He took two boxes of corned beef cans, one box of tomatoes, canned, one crate of . . ."

The telephone rang. I glanced at my watch as I went over to it. It was four o'clock. A man snapped an inquiry for Lieutenant Marsh. I called Eddie.

"Marsh! . . . yes, Briggs . . . where? . . . wait a minute. Doc! Get some clothes on . . . hurry . . . Briggs, listen! Put the Panty Burke description out again fast . . . and get a man up there and tell him not to leave her alone a minute until I get there. Hop to it! I won't be ten minutes."

I was throwing on clothes in the bedroom and didn't ask anything until I got to my coat. When I went back into the living room, Eddie was ready and pacing around. He said, "Come on, kid, let's go!"

While we were waiting for the elevator I asked him what was up.

"It's Grace Larkin. She's in Bellevue . . ."

"What happened?"

"Some guy damned near beat her to death about an hour ago."

12

We decided there wasn't any use hanging around Bellevue and headed for One Hundred Sixty-ninth where Grace Larkin had been attacked. She had been slugged several times over the head with something like a sap and wouldn't answer any questions for some time. There was no outward evidence of fracture but they were taking her to x-ray as we left.

There was a lot of fancy driving and very little talking on the way uptown. A couple of police cars were parked in front of the place when we braked up, and I could make out cops moving around in their lights. A spot was turned on the steps of the house. We went up.

Eddie walked past the uniformed man on the door and said, "Who's in charge?" The man said, "Sergeant Welsh, sir."

"Good. Where is he?"

"Second floor, in the back, Lieutenant."

We hustled up the stairs and found Welsh and another detective in a room which, at another time, would have been very attractive—chintz or something on the furniture and at the windows. As it was, the place was a wreck. It had been turned upside down by somebody who wanted something badly and didn't give a damn how he got it. Eddie said:

"Hello, Welsh, you know Doc Connor?"

"Sure. Hello, Doctor."

The other detective said, "This is the place we were looking for, Lieutenant, the dressmaker's name is Perry. She's downstairs."

"Thanks for the tip, Jake." Eddie grinned at the younger man. "How'd you find it so fast?" The guy got red and shuffled his feet.

"Well, naturally I . . ."

"Forget it, Jake. I was kidding." He turned to Welsh. "What happened here, Paddy?"

"Sometime after three o'clock, the woman, Mrs. Perry, thought she heard somebody moving around upstairs. It woke her up. She called up to the Larkin girl—she's the only one in the house right now although the old lady has roomers most of the time. Well, she called and didn't get any answer. Then she stepped out in the hall and looked up. There wasn't any light up there and she couldn't hear anything, so she went back to bed."

"Is her bedroom under this one?"

"No. It's on the other side. There's a kind of a parlor under this room; the bedroom over Mrs. Perry's is not occupied."

I said that Mrs. Perry wouldn't have a roomer in the house under the circumstances and Eddie said that's right, of course. Eddie looked over the room as Welsh talked. It was searched all right . . . even to the inside of the mattress.

"She couldn't go to sleep, though, because she was scared. After a while she heard somebody scrape a foot on the little fire escape that comes down out back and then heard the gate at the alley creak a little. She went to the front window of the parlor and saw somebody—she thought it was a man—hurrying across the street. She stood in the hall, then, and hollered for Grace Larkin. No answer. She went upstairs and tried the door and it was locked from the inside—nobody answered when she pounded. Then she ran out to the saloon at the corner and called the police."

"Who got here first?"

"Car 73, Ferguson and Payne, they're out front if you want them."

"Yeah. Get them." Eddie wandered around the room. "They were looking for something pretty small, Doc." He picked up a compact. The back had been pried off it. "Small and flat."

"Like what?"

"Oh, like a lot of things—a folded piece of paper, maybe, or a photograph. It could have been a key."

I wondered what my corrugated box could have held that fit that description. I wondered, too, how much hell I would get from Eddie for holding that out on him. I'd have to let him have the stuff today for sure. The two officers came pounding up the stairs and into the room. One of them said yessir.

"What did you find here?"

"The woman said the door was locked so we came up the fire escape. There was no light in the room and we turned it on. Then Payne went back to stand by at the car. I found the girl on the floor by the bed, right here, her hands and feet were tied with wire and she had a washcloth stuffed in her mouth. Her nose was bleeding and her head was cut."

"Did you untie her right away?"

"Yes, sir. The wire is there on the bureau."

"Okay, what then?"

"That was all for us, sir. The ambulance and Detective Sergeant Welsh got here about the same time, very quick, and I went below."

"That's it, eh? All right. Thanks." Eddie turned to Welsh. "I guess you know that this is our baby, don't you, Paddy?"

"Oh, sure. It's the Panty Burke case, isn't it?"

"That's right, and if my guess is any good, the guy's desperate for something his girl had of his, something that would fit in this . . ." Eddie held up the compact. "I can't see that it's so very important because we've got more evidence on the guy than we need now. But it might be. Let's find it."

"Right, Eddie. We'll get it if it's here."

"I want to talk to the woman downstairs and get back downtown. Jake, you stick around."

"Okay, Lieutenant."

Mrs. Perry proved to be a substantial old gal who showed a tendency to be cagey about Grace Larkin's visit. Eddie was polite enough but kept at her. Did anyone ever visit Larkin? No. Did she receive any letters? No. Did she tell you she was in trouble? Mrs. Perry hadn't asked her. It was none of her business

if she were. She had sewn for Grace Larkin and liked her. If she
wanted to come and stay a few nights with her . . .

Eddie waved his hand like a brakeman stopping a freight.
"Mrs. Perry. Wait a minute and listen to me. I believe that you
know as well as we do that Grace Larkin was in a lot of trouble,
that she wanted to hide. Now get this through your head. Grace
was not hiding from us, from the police. Did you know that?"

"No. I didn't."

"Well, it's true. She was hiding from just what happened to
her last night, and what may happen to her again if she ever gets
out on the street again."

"*That's* not true."

"Why?"

"Because . . . well she *was* hiding from the police. And not
for anything that she'd done, either."

I said, "I know that, Mrs. Perry, she told me that. She called
me last night. She was hiding with you because the man she
loved was in trouble. Is that right?

"Yes. That's right." The old lady took up the cudgels. "And
if you think that the man who hurt her so last night was the
man she loved, you're wrong."

I said I thought so, too. Eddie grunted and settled down to
some more questions that got him no place. After a while he
said let's go back downtown and we went out to the car. It still
wasn't daylight when we stopped at Bellevue.

Grace Larkin had been given sedation and was sleeping. The
x-ray had shown no fractures. She had not regained proper consciousness but had become extremely restless. That was all. We
went on to my place and Eddie came up and flopped down in
my big chair. He looked pretty beat and I went out and put
some coffee on. I heard him dial the phone and talk to his
office. Checking. Pounding along in a tired, monotonous, com-
petent way that made me ache for the guy.

I came back with the coffee and said Merry Christmas. Eddie
grinned and said, "Yeah. That's right. Merry Christmas to you."

"Want a present?"

"For my stocking?" That broke me up. I looked at those feet and thought of the box Larkin had sent me. "What the hell are you laughing at? My feet again?"

"Sorry, Eddie . . . but yes."

"I'm in no mood for gags."

"It isn't a gag. I've got something for you that might turn out to be quite a present." I went into the office and brought out the carton. "After what I saw tonight, I think this stuff may answer a lot of questions."

"What is it?"

"Surprise! Look and see." I didn't feel that cute. I dreaded the next five minutes. Eddie dug into the box.

"Doc!" Even though I'd been waiting for it, it startled me.

"What, Eddie?"

"When did you get hold of this stuff?"

"When? . . . or where?"

"Dammit, don't horse around. I can guess where you got it. I want to know *when* . . . how long have you had these things?"

"Since late yesterday afternoon. I got a locker key in the mail and Katie and I got the box from Grand Central. I was going to show it to you last night . . ."

"The hell you were!"

"The hell I wasn't. Listen, Eddie, the girl . . . well what's the use of arguing? Here's her note. You can add that to the collection."

Eddie grabbed the letter out of my hand. "I won't stand for this sort of thing! This is police business, not yours. Dammit-to-hell, this is my job!"

"You asked me for help, didn't you?"

"I asked you to ask a couple of questions of your tramp friends around here . . . and I ought to have my head examined for doing it."

The guy got up and put on his coat, shaking his head like a bull. I didn't say anything. I was too sore. He jammed his hat on his head and picked up the box.

"Why don't you get wise to yourself instead of being a meddlesome playboy all your life? This girl might not have been assaulted . . ."

"Why, goddammit, you . . ."

"Don't goddammit me! Just keep out of my business from now on and I'll damned well keep out of yours." He started out, then turned back. "You got anything else on this case that belongs to me?"

"You can start keeping out of my business right now, flatfoot, if I have anything else for the cops I'll give it to your boss!"

"If you've got anything else for the cops I'll come up here and slap it out of you. That's a promise."

"Why don't you go home?"

He stormed out. I heard the elevator rattle down and looked out the window at the first light of the morning. I guess I was shaking some. I watched him come out and go across the street to his car with his big package—that silly old brown hat of his on sideways and all out of shape. The stupid lug!

The apartment seemed empty as hell.

I put away the glasses and the turkey and fretted around getting ready for bed. I said "So what?" quite a few times, mostly out loud. It wasn't even convincing. Finally I went to bed and after a while I got to sleep.

At ten o'clock the phone rang and Katie said, "Aren't you up yet, darling? It's ten already . . . and it's Christmas!"

13

From there on, all I got was what I read in the papers—which wasn't much. The Larkin story was related in some detail and, of course, tied up with the search for Burke. The grocery robbery was included in all the roundup stories. The guy had stolen enough stuff to stay indoors for the rest of the winter.

I wouldn't think of the killer as Panty Burke any more so I called him Maximilian Wardhouse—Max. Max was the guy they ought to go after. Burke never cuffed Grace Larkin around like that. Burke didn't want anything from Larkin he couldn't have had for the asking.

Another thing I decided about Max was that New York was too hot for him. He'd exposed himself for the last time he dared or, at least, he couldn't count on that sort of luck much longer. It seemed pretty certain to me that Max would either be holed up where they'd have to dig him out or would have to get out of town. The groceries suggested holing up. The use of the truck only for an hour suggested the hideout was close. Yet the stuff could have simply been transferred to a car and taken to the mountains, or anyplace.

That sort of thing had been running through my mind for twenty-four hours. I didn't talk much about it to Katie, that evening, when we had Christmas dinner together. I felt rotten about Eddie and didn't feel like discussing it. Not even with Katie.

It was Friday morning, two days after Christmas, that I voted everybody out of the picture except Maximilian Wardhouse and Midge Manson. The villains of the piece. Every

policeman in New York was looking for Panty Burke and nobody was looking for Maximilian. Nobody was paying much
attention, either, to the nasty little woman up in Boston who
could have killed Peters.

I tried to see Grace Larkin and got shut out. Nobody was
permitted to visit the patient. The interne on the floor, when
he found out I was a physician, confided that it was the police
and that they'd had a cop there night and day. He also confided
that the patient was conscious, rational and had talked with the
police at length. He was an eager, nice kid and I gave him the
look-me-up-we'll-have-lunch.

There was to be a pretty fair sort of a fight at the Garden
that night and I wandered over to Jacobs Beach to hear the
gossip. I caught a glimpse of Stirnie Maize halfway down the
block, caught his glance as he looked half over his shoulder. He
scuttled away, queer for him if he had anything to peddle. I decided to find him. After all it had been Stirnie who sent Grace
Larkin to me.

But he was gone. "He was around here a while ago, Doc . . ."
It was either that or, "Stirnie? He ought to be around someplace, he always is." I got curious.

Yeah. It had been Stirnie who sent Grace to me. Stirnie who
had gone to great lengths to tell me what a heel Burke was. The
little chiseler had known a great deal about Midge: the story of
the hocked ring, the story of her hard luck, the details of how
her husband died. He had seemed perfectly willing to get me
her Boston address and knew where to look for it.

I caught up with him in a bar up Eighth Avenue a way. He
was having a bowl of chile in a booth by himself, stooped over
it and messing his chin. His left hand was full of crackers.

"Hello, Stirnie." He looked up fish-eyed and wiped his chin
with the back of his cracker fist. He swallowed a couple of
times—once to get the food down, then once on the house.

"Why hello, Doc! Haven't seen you for quite a while. Are
you going to the fights?"

"Maybe. Can I sit down with you?"

"I was just about finished, Doc . . ."

"That's all right. I won't hold you up. I just want to ask a couple of questions." He resumed eating with his head down close to the bowl. I couldn't see his face. I waited.

"Sure, Doc. What kinda questions?"

"Has anybody from the Detective Bureau been talking to you lately, Stirnie? Eddie Marsh or any of his bunch?" He put his head back in his bowl.

"Detective Bureau! Why would they be talking to me?"

"I thought they might have asked what you knew about Panty Burke—and Ernie Peters." His left hand opened slowly and the crackers dribbled out on the checked tablecloth.

"I don't know nothing about either of them."

"You told me plenty about Burke . . ."

"Nothing the cops'd want. What you trying to make of it, Doc?"

"You heard about Grace Larkin . . ."

"About Burke beating her up? Yeah. I heard about it." He seemed relieved at the turn of the talk. "He took a hell of a chance for a guy wanted for murder." "What makes you think it was Burke?"

"Are you kidding? It had to be."

"That isn't quite true. As a matter of fact, it could have been anybody as far as the evidence goes."

"Yeah? Like who?"

"Like anybody we haven't yet connected with the deals the Burke-Larkin-Peters team had going. Like Maximilian Wardhouse."

"I never heard of the guy."

Maize carefully put the spilled crackers back in his almost empty bowl. He mixed them thoroughly to wet them. I waited until he'd shoveled in the first mouthful.

"Seen Midge Manson lately?" I expected the crackers full in the face . . . and they damned near came. Stirnie's cheeks bulged and his face reddened with the restraint. He choked the stuff down.

"Seen her, you say?"

"Yeah." I couldn't help grinning at the guy. "I just asked."

"Hell, no. I haven't seen her."

"You knew she'd been in town, of course . . ."

"Maybe you'd tell me how I'd know when she was in town."

"Yeah, Stirnie, maybe I will." He squirmed. "You see, you were good enough to get Midge's address for me. Right?"

"Why sure, Doc, I just happened to know how to get it."

"That's right. You got it from the guy that made the loan on the ring. Right?"

"That's right."

"Didn't he tell you that Midge had already redeemed the ring when you talked to him?"

I've never seen a man look more—what would it be?—more cornered, I guess. Yet it needn't have meant a thing. I suppose the little rat spent most of his life in a corner, fearing something, if only hunger. He ate that way. I didn't need an answer.

"Do you know what day she was in town, Stirnie?"

"What day?"

"The day Ernie Peters was killed." I got up. "Thanks, pal, I'll see you later."

"Yeah. Okay, Doc."

The air in Eighth Avenue smelled fresh and good—and that, brother, is a commentary on the air where I'd been. As a candidate for Maximilian, Maize didn't show much promise, but as chief ferret and woman-beater . . . could be. Stirnie was another guy who was too anxious for me to believe all the obvious facts, too quick to help me arrive at all the obvious conclusions. That could have been.

Which, of course, would let Midge Manson shoot Peters. She would not have had to be in New York for any of the rest. No reason why Stirnie's footprints wouldn't work, the ones at the Peters scene and those in the for-rent truck. Burke's fingerprints could have been in that room all the time. He could have hidden there or, possibly, been held there.

Always, however, taking *my* case rather than the police's, based on the hypothesis that Burke hadn't killed Peters.

I forgot the fight and walked back to my place trying to figure out why I shouldn't go to Boston again. The old hunch came back to me with a surge. The answers were up in that shoddy little room where the baby-faced widow lived.

I called up Katie, packed a fairly big bag and dialed the New Haven about trains. A rummage through the desk located my gun-toting permit, a merit-badge for my help in the Harry Lennen business. I have never had any use for the permit nor the neat, flat .32 automatic it specified. It seemed a little silly—but the whole thing seemed silly—except that people in the case had already been killed and slugged for knowing too much about something or somebody. Maybe they might think I knew too much, too.

I slept at the Copley again that night.

"Wickland Street," said the porter, "is not a nice neighborhood. Right here, where you indicate" (his stubby finger held the point on the city map), "would be thirty-seven."

I told him I'd been there once before but wanted to get a little more information on the neighborhood. I must have worn a professional air or something because he asked me if I was a detective and we exchanged wise-guy leers. "From New York," I told him.

"Well, sir, the section is like most of the houses left near the water in that area. It's pretty shoddy. It's been several generations since those houses were stylish—and quite a lot of years since most of them have been anything but tenements."

"I see. There seems to be quite a little business section not far from there . . . I walked only a few blocks to find a cab."

"That's Hartville Road. The business section depends more on through traffic than on the poorer side-streets. I got a friend tends bar just up from where you're going."

"Yeah? Where?"

Then he told me about Pat Harold. Promised to call him up and set me in. I tipped him and suggested he make the call soon. A local bar might be a good spot to headquarter, especially if the barman thought I was a detective.

After lunch I took a cab to Hartville Road and got off a block past the bar and walked back to look the place over. A sign said "Hartville Grill." Just a place, like a thousand others. A tough-looking egg was wiping glasses behind the bar. I walked in and asked where the men's room was. The guy nodded his head toward the back without slowing down on the job.

The can was clean and fresh. I figured that would be all right if I had to hole up in there for a while sometime. When I went back into the bar, the guy was still polishing. He looked up at me without a word and I said, "Old Forester." He went down below and hunted it up . . . it's a little on the choosey side for the neighborhood.

"Water?"

"Yes, thanks."

That was it. There was the whisky . . . there was the water . . . there was old silent Sam washing the dishes. I led off.

"You Pat Harold?"

"Yeah."

"Man call you about me?"

"Yeah."

"I need some help. I'm not sure you know anything that will do me any good, but, from a look at your place, here, I'm sure that nobody that means anything to you is concerned. What do you say?"

"What do you want to know?"

"Know a woman by the name of Midge Manson?" Pat didn't blink.

"Yeah. She used to come in here. Haven't seen her lately."

"How long since she's been in?" He had to think this over.

"Maybe October sometime—in the fall anyway."

"Did she come in alone?"

"Not that I remember. Always with her husband."

"Do you recall much about him, the husband?"

"He was a drunk—died of it, they say."

"That's right. Tell me, Pat, did you ever see the woman with anybody else?"

"She come in once with a man, a big man. Last time I seen her. They sat in one of the booths and talked. I brought the drinks to the table. The man wore a gun on him, in a shoulder holster. I saw it when I leant over him."

"When was this?"

"It was right after I heard her husband died. She hadn't been in for quite a while. Then she come in with this fella."

"Was he a sort of a good-looking mug in a blue suit?"

"Yeah. Come to think of it."

"Broken-down old brown hat?" Pat nodded, leaning across the bar with excitement. "Yeah! That's the guy."

"Okay. Thanks, Pat." I finished my drink. "If you happen to see him around again, keep an eye on him for me."

"I sure will, Mister. You think he might come in, eh?"

"I'm sure he'll be in the neighborhood before long. See you around, Pat."

"Right, sir. Come in again."

As I walked down the street, I wondered how soon Eddie Marsh would be back to Boston. It wouldn't be long, now.

14

The alley ran across the back of the fat woman's house—directly under Midge Manson's window. It was just after midnight and there were no lights showing in the place. I pressed my back against the low garage building, opposite, and waited.

I was waiting because I felt pretty certain Midge would come out again sometime during the night. Also, I sensed that it wouldn't be more than a day or two until the payoff, whatever that would be.

It had been this way.

At five-thirty I'd watched Midge come out of the place she worked. She was carrying a small bag. She hurried down the street and into the drugstore at the corner, straight to a phone booth, where she spent several minutes. I could see, through the window, that she didn't pick up the receiver, but stood in the booth looking at her watch. After a while the phone must have rung because she hurriedly grabbed the instrument and started talking without stopping to dial any number.

She came directly out of the drugstore and walked quickly through several blocks to an auto supply place. I got a good look at what she did there because the store was small and the window faced the single counter. She hauled a piece of paper out of her purse and showed it to the clerk. He referred to a catalogue of some sort and went into the back of the store. After a while, he came back with a box from which he took something. I couldn't make it out. Midge put the stuff in her small case, paid the man and left.

I let her go and waited a few minutes. The clerk was getting ready to shut the place up when I went in. He said, "Hello. You just got in under the wire. What can I do for you?"

"I thought I might catch my wife here. She was to get some stuff for me. Short, blonde woman. Probably had a small traveling bag with her."

"She just left a minute before you came in. Packard manifold gaskets?"

I said, "Yeah. That's right. She get 'em?"

"Yes. I just happened to have a set in stock. Fellow ordered them and never came back. We don't usually stock parts for the old models."

"I can understand that. Not much call for stuff that out of date."

"Oh, I wouldn't say that. There are a lot of 1939 Packards on the road yet. It's just that we're not a very big outfit and can't carry everything."

"Well, thanks a lot. I'm glad she got them okay."

When I left, the guy was turning out the lights. I grabbed a cab and headed for Hartville Road. I got out before we reached the corner of Wickland Street, figuring Midge would probably come home on a bus. I damned near ran into her as she turned into a liquor store just ahead of me.

So little Midge was riding taxicabs nowadays! She was still carrying her small case and, presumably, the Packard gaskets. She bought two bottles of whisky, put them in the bag and headed home.

From half a block away I saw her go into the house and I decided to get something to eat before she made up her mind to come out again. I waited long enough for her to come out if she were simply going to clean up and go some place, and then left.

I got sort of a steak at a dog-wagon on Hartville Road and thought a lot about that 1939 Packard which was getting an overhauling somewhere. Certainly nobody connected with the case owned it legally or the police would have known something about it. It could be important.

So I'd spent the next five hours waiting around the neighborhood for Midge to deliver those gaskets some place. It could be the garage building at my back. I had a nasty moment thinking about that but decided the place was too close and forgot it.

All of a sudden the back door scraped a little and I retreated as far as I could into the deep shadow of the building. It was Midge. I recognized her small figure as she turned and shut the door behind her. When she walked quietly down toward the mouth of the alley, I could see that she was carrying the bag. She stopped and watched the street carefully before she stepped out. Apparently the police weren't keeping a man on all night. At least nobody followed her.

I let her get well into the street before I went after her. She was walking briskly when I saw her—almost halfway down to Hartville Road. She cut across the street and into an alley on the other side. I ducked in and could see her, silhouetted against the streetlight at the other end.

A cold wind blew up the alley from the bay and I bent my head for a moment against its sting. When I looked up, the girl had disappeared. I stopped short and stepped into a doorway. She couldn't have made the end of the alley and must have stepped into an entry as I had. As I was pretty sure she hadn't seen me, I figured that was where she was going. On the other hand, maybe she'd heard someone coming and hidden. After about twenty seconds I saw her appear again, carrying the bag as before. I followed as carefully as I could, but was afraid to let her get too far ahead. She got to the end of the alley just as I passed the doorway where she'd stood. Before she went on out into the lighted street beyond, she turned and looked back. I sidestepped into the doorway and somebody slugged me.

I hit the deck hard and the guy tripped over me as he jumped out of the entry. I tried to hang onto his leg and he sapped me again and ran like hell. By the time I got over being sick and climbed back to my feet, there wasn't a sound any place. The alley was deserted.

I staggered back to Hartville Road and into the bar. Pat Harold was still there and half a dozen men were sitting around.

Pat set the Forester out and said, "You got blood on your face. What happened to you?"

"I got in an argument." I threw down a drink and went back to the washroom. There was some sort of a cut on my scalp and I mopped it up. Nothing much. Well, at least I'd been closer to the killer than Marsh ever had. It was all here, all of it. There wasn't anything left for Eddie in New York. Midge and Maximilian.

When I came back into the bar I felt some better. I sat down and Pat came over. He didn't say anything, but set out a drink and waited for me to open up.

Always topside in my mind was the thought that I'd better tell somebody what I knew—Eddie Marsh, probably. Maybe the Boston cops, but that would amount to the same thing. Certainly I was getting too close for a civilian, or whatever you call people who aren't cops.

Pat was still standing by. I said, "Pat, do you know anybody around here with an old Packard?"

"An old Packard." He looked at the wall over my head for a moment. "No, Mister, I don't. I don't know anybody around here with any kind of a Packard at all." He wiped the bar in front of me. "Why? You looking for one?"

"In a way, yes."

"There's a fella comes in here who wants to sell his 1943 Buick pretty reasonable . . ." Pat was looking thoughtfully out the front window. "Hey! There's the woman you was asking about . . . out in front. Buying a paper."

Midge Manson was putting a newspaper under her arm. She exchanged a word or two with the boy and turned as if to come in. I picked up my drink and looked around for a booth. I told Pat to say nothing about anybody asking for her. He said, "Your head's bleedin' again. Maybe you better go back in the can."

I told him to hell with it and that the chances were I wanted to talk to her anyway, I slid over to a back booth and sat down just as she came in the door. She went up to the bar where Pat was and said something. He reached back for a bottle and poured her a drink. She'd apparently been home because she had left the small bag she'd been carrying. That would make sense. She'd turn the two trips out into one—just tell the landlady she went down to the corner for a drink.

Pat left her immediately and walked down the bar. She gulped down the drink and called him back. He talked a little more with a couple of guys where he was and walked slowly back and poured her another drink, without saying anything as nearly as I could make out. I watched carefully to see if there was going to be any conversation. There wasn't. Pat went back to his friends. Midge needed a couple of drinks, I guess. There would be no doubt of the fact that the guy that slugged me had raced out of the alley and caught up with her . . . at least long enough to holler trouble and beat it.

I couldn't see her face in the mirror so I knew she couldn't see me. I felt the blood leaking through my hair again and daubed at it with my handkerchief.

After what seemed a long while, Midge flagged Pat again and I heard her say something about one for the road so I got set. I didn't see any percentage in chasing her again because she'd probably go right home. On the other hand there might be another slug over the head, or even better, waiting outside for me. I wished for a cop or two.

Pat poured the drink and picked up some money. I heard the register ring and Midge tilted her head back—once, quick, set the glass down and picked up her change. As she turned, I raised my own drink and used it to hide my face. I felt her moving away from the bar. As I bent my head down again, I saw her feet start—and stop. The feet came straight toward my booth and I looked up.

"Hello, Doc." Here it was. Her voice was very quiet. "How'd you cut your head? It's bleeding."

"Hello, Midge." Pretty casual talk but you could feel the tension under the words. God knows I didn't feel like running into any more of her boy friends tonight. "Some lug tried to rob me a while ago. I didn't like it and he slugged me with a sap."

"This isn't a nice neighborhood at night. Can I sit down?"

"Sure. I was about to order another drink. Will you join me?"

"Why not?" She moved in opposite me and I called Pat. While the big barman was getting the drinks, she said, "What you doing in Boston, Doc?"

"I came back to see you."

"Yeah?" She showed no surprise at that. "I hear your friend Grace Larkin got herself into some more trouble."

"She did. Somebody beat her up."

"Your head's bleeding pretty badly. Maybe Pat's got a first-aid kit around some place. I could put a patch on it."

I daubed again with my handkerchief and a mess of blood came away. Pat came back with the drinks. The girl said, "You got a first-aid kit, Pat?"

"Yeah. I got one in back. Want I should bring it out, Mister?"

I said sure go ahead. Midge said, "Bring a double jigger of gin, too."

Pat went on his way and I asked the woman what the gin was for. She gave me a funny look and said, "You ought to know, Doc, or didn't you ever do any barroom surgery?"

I said oh and she dug into her bag for a pair of manicure scissors. When Pat came back with the stuff, she stuck her scissors into the gin and left them there while she opened the kit. She handled the sterpad like an outfielder handles a fly ball. The adhesive she tore in strips and stuck the ends of it to the edge of the table. She took the shade off the light and said, "Okay, Doc."

I didn't want her to whack off as much hair as I would have if it had been a patient of mine—and said so.

"Let's look at it." I bent my head over the table toward her. "You must've scared the guy."

"What guy?"

"The guy that tried to rob you. He really bopped you. Wait a minute . . ." She looked some more. "You'll either have a patch of hair off or you'll have to wear a bow under your chin. You can't leave that open." I moved my head and she got hold of an ear. "It really ought to have a suture." She took the scissors out of the gin and wiped them with a piece of sterile gauze, wrapping them in it and laying them aside. Then she sopped my head with gin soaked into cotton. It stung like hell. When she'd finished, she started snipping with her scissors. She was quick and sure. Five minutes later she was through. She said, "Let it alone for a couple of days. It'll heal all right. I pulled the edges together with adhesive."

Pat took the stuff away and brought us a couple of drinks. The girl had a mocking little smile on her baby face.

"Neat, eh?"

"Yeah. Thanks." I grinned back a little. "Where'd you learn it?"

I thought she looked startled for a moment. Then she said, "I took a Red Cross course during the war. A lot of women did."

"You worked so efficiently I thought you might have been a nurse at some time or other."

"I was in show business."

"So Stirnie Maize said."

She did look startled then. "Stirnie Maize . . . where does he come in?"

"Frankly, I don't know. He just said that."

"Oh." Nobody said anything for a while. The, bells were clanging away in the back of my head and I knew damned well that I'd be asking for real trouble if I didn't watch my step. Somewhere within a few blocks there was an exceedingly tough guy who wanted me strictly out of his business and apparently didn't care much how he got me out of it. His name was Maximilian—or Burke or Maize—it didn't make much difference. I didn't want any more of him that night and I decided to fold it up and go back to the hotel.

Midge Manson drank her whisky and looked up suddenly. "Tell me, Doc, where do you come into all this?"

"All what?" It was silly but I couldn't think of anything else to say. She sighed and looked impatient.

"Look. You were here the other day asking me questions about Panty Burke. You said you were a friend of Grace Larkin's. She'd disappeared. You wanted to find her. Now you've found her. Now you're back in Boston and say you want to talk to me." Her washy blue eyes were dirty-hard. "Now, what the hell do you want?"

I think she was holding her breath after that. But she wasn't scared. There wasn't much of a corner for me to duck into, but one thing was sure—it was time for me to duck. I still had to get back to the hotel and, whatever Midge's connection with the case, she didn't want me around and had somebody to back her up.

I said, "It's simple enough. I'm trying to find out who damned nearly beat Grace Larkin to death."

"Burke you mean—you're trying to find Burke."

"I don't think so. I don't think Burke would have done it."

"Yes. He would have and he did. You're trying to find Burke for the cops. You worked on a cop case before. I read about it."

"It's this way, put it this way. I think Larkin got a bad break. I think you got a bad break. I've got an idea that, somewhere back in your head, you've got the knowledge that would turn up a really nasty guy . . . maybe something you've forgotten. Maybe something you don't even know you know."

"So that's the way it is." The woman began to slip her coat over her shoulders. "All right, Doc, I'll tell you again. I don't know anything about what kind of a break Grace Larkin got but you and the cops and everybody else know I got a bad break. I've tried to live my own life here and to forget about it. The police have let me do it. I answered their questions and they went away satisfied. Now you come around and start it all over again. Listen. I don't know anything about any of it. I don't want to know anything about it. Grace Larkin knows the whole story and I think she's into it up to her neck. Somebody beat her up to keep her quiet."

Midge stood up. "I'm going home, now, and I don't want to be bothered by you, or anybody else, any more. Get that through your head—what's left of it." She glanced at her handiwork on my skull. "Get out of my affairs, Doc, and stay out."

Then she drank the sterile gin and was gone. Pat came over with another drink which, he explained, was on the house. I drank it as he stood around like a pup in the kitchen when you're cutting up meat for a stew. I thanked him and paid my bill. He said, "Get anything?"

I told him yeah, a warning to get out of town. There was a cab on the corner and as I piled in the man said, "Watch your head." It struck me funny because I hadn't been able to get my hat on as it was.

There was a note in my box at the Copley.

15

The note had said, "Doc: I am in room five-eleven. Please call me when you come in, regardless of how late." It was signed by Grace Larkin.

I looked at my watch. It was after two. There were a lot of youngsters running around the lobby, most of them in formal clothes. I figured there had to be a cop there some place. Grace Larkin was only just out of the hospital and they'd never let her go unchaperoned. There were a few guys standing around and some sitting reading newspapers like the detectives in stories. I didn't see any faces I knew.

On a hunch I went over to the information and mail window and asked the girl if Mr. Edward Marsh had arrived yet. She consulted a rotary gimmick and said yes, he was registered.

"I don't want to bother him now but I'd like his room number."

"Are you a guest of the hotel?"

"Yes. I'm Dr. Connor in room nine-sixteen."

"Mr. Marsh is in room five-ten, sir."

"Thanks." I might have known. Right across the hall from Grace. Eddie had brought her to Boston, or followed her there. His identification card would have got him the room he wanted. I called room five-eleven.

"Grace?" Her voice sounded tense and weary. "This is Doc."

"Where are you?"

"In the lobby. Look here. Did Eddie Marsh bring you to Boston?"

"No. He doesn't know I'm here. I slipped out by way of . . ."

"I see. Did they tell you that you could leave town?"

"They didn't tell me anything. They just turned me loose."

". . . and followed you."

"What do you mean?"

"I mean that Eddie Marsh is in the room across the hall from you right now."

"He's . . ."

"Yes. In five-ten." She made small noises I couldn't understand. "Now listen, Grace, tell me something. It's pretty damned important."

"I'll tell you."

"Why did you come here?"

"Oh God, Doc! There's no answer anywhere else. Pike Manson's wife has to know something about Panty. There's no one else left."

"The papers said you couldn't recognize the person who slugged you. Is that true?"

"Yes. It was a man—from his clothing and his strength. That's all I know." She paused. "Doc. What are you doing in Boston?"

"The same thing you're doing. I'm convinced it's all here. There's nothing left for us in New York. I've talked to Midge Manson. It didn't get me anyplace. I've learned a couple of things, though."

"How can I see you?"

"Tonight?"

"Of course. I won't have a chance in the morning."

"If I know Marsh you haven't got a chance now. Open your door a crack, quietly, and look at Marsh's door. I'll hold on."

I heard her set the instrument down and waited. Pretty soon she came back. She spoke very cautiously.

"Doc." I asked her what? "His door was open and the room was dark. But the minute my door opened he asked me if I wanted anything. I pretended to be surprised and told him I was nervous. He said to go back to sleep—he'd be watching."

"He would be." I knew damned well, what he was looking

for. Not the guy to come back and beat her up again. The lug was waiting for me. All the feeling I'd had about our row dissolved comfortably. To hell with him. "Well, that's that, Grace. He's not going to let you out of his sight. Whatever business we do will have to be on the telephone."

"What do you want to know, Doc?"

"Several things. Did you lock your door?"

"Yes. And the transom is closed."

"Good. Marsh and I aren't getting along and I've got to keep out of his way."

"I know. It was about Panty's things, wasn't it?" I told her that was most of it and she went on. "He gave me hell, too, for that. He said he didn't know why he hadn't thrown us both into the jug so he could do his work without interference!"

"To hell with him. Tell me. Did you give the police any information I don't already know?"

"Not as much. There were a million small details about the night the man broke in, but they didn't amount to anything. Of course they pounded and pounded on what the man might have been looking for, but I couldn't help them."

"Couldn't, Grace, or wouldn't?"

She hesitated so long that I asked her what was the matter. Then she said, "I don't know, Doc." She sounded bitterly tired. "I don't know."

"You mean you don't know whether you could have helped the police or not . . . whether you knew what the guy was after?"

"No. I don't know whether . . . I don't know what to do about something. Oh hell, Doc! There isn't anyone else I can trust. I do know what he was after . . . at least I think I do."

"What?"

"I don't know whether I should tell you or not . . . and I'm afraid to tell you over the phone. The line could be tapped or the operator listening in or anything."

I thought a second and got an idea. "You can be sure the line's not tapped, but okay, write it in a note. In about five minutes a boy will be up with a package of aspirin. Send the note back by him. I'll see the boy first."

"All right, Doc. I have only one thing to ask about it. If the thing I have in my possession will help Panty, I want it to go to the police. If it won't . . . Oh damn it, Doc. You'll have to understand. It was his last confidence. . . . It was the only thing he ever asked me to do for him . . . in a business way, that is. I feel like I was selling him out."

"Grace. If Panty killed Peters, nothing will save him. Marsh will get him sooner or later. On the other hand, I'm doing all this snooping around because—like you—I have a hunch he was the victim of some sort of a frameup. Marsh and I had a hell of a row on Christmas and I'm not giving him anything. I'm certain that Panty wouldn't have left anything with you which would involve either of you in anything. On the other hand, he might have left something with you which would have kept him, and you, out of such an involvement. See?"

"Okay. Send the boy, Doc. And thanks."

"Forget it, kid. Keep your chin up. I'll see you when I can."

I hung up and went off looking for a boy. There was one at the porter's desk, studying a *Racing Form*. I asked him if he knew where he could get some aspirin and would he do a private errand for me. He looked interested.

"They always got aspirin in the bar, sir."

"Right. I've got a friend, my lady friend, in five-eleven who's got a headache and can't sleep. She also wants to send me down a note, kind of private like. Get it?"

He got it. Grinned. "Sure."

"See if you can get a box of aspirin from the bar and I'll meet you at the elevator bank before you go up. There's a fin in it."

"Right. Okay, big shot, you bought something." He beat it. I saw a big pair of shoulders leaning over the desk that had cop written across the back of them. I looked at his shoes. Check. The man went to the house phones and got a number. He talked a minute and went over to the elevators. After he got in I watched the indicator. Five . . . five right. Maybe Eddie wanted some sleep.

The boy came back with a box of aspirin on a tray. A bare tray. I sent him back to the bar for a napkin. "The aspirin comes off the tray and the note goes on, see? Under the napkin."

"Romantic."

"Yes. Isn't it!" I thought I'd better set him right. "On the other hand, pally, if you see a very large gent in a blue suit around there, it may be less romantic . . . so take it easy."

He gave me a very thoughtful and very Massachusetts ayah. "I see. Now the five bucks makes sense."

I spent a long five minutes behind a column, expecting Marsh and his relief man to bring the boy back by the ear, but the lad spilled out of the elevator alone. He spotted me and didn't give me a tumble but went over to the porter's desk. There was a pad on the desk and the boy rather pointedly stuck an envelope between the leaves. Then he glanced at me and crossed the lobby. Stood there with his back to me. I waited a while and split my attention between the down-coming elevators and the porter's desk until I saw the big cop come out of the elevator. He looked around the lobby and went out. I waited a little longer and the boy came over.

"The big guy was up there all right."

"The one that just went out?"

"Yeah. And another one in a bathrobe. They were across the hall. Cops, weren't they?"

"Private detectives, I think."

The boy frowned. "Oh, it's that way."

"I'm afraid so." He looked uncomfortable when I admitted they were detectives.

"I wouldn't want to get into trouble. I thought it was just a sort of, you know, romance."

"Don't worry. That's what it was. There won't be any trouble."

"They asked me questions."

"What questions?"

"They asked what I was bringing up to five-eleven. They come out of five-ten and asked. I showed them and they went back. The note's on the porter's desk. No, sir. I wouldn't want to do anything wrong."

"You didn't, kid, and thanks. Here's the fin."

"Okay, thank you, Mister." He started away and turned back. "I guess you know this is one of the finest hotels in the country, don't you?"

"Sure I do, and I know you like your job. You just did a guy a nice favor. I can't get in touch with her any other way and you helped me out."

"Yeah. All right. So long, sir."

I walked casually over to the porter's desk and took the note out of the pad. I stuck it into my pocket and headed for a far corner of the lobby where I could see in all directions and get away if it became necessary. I opened the envelope.

> Doc:
> Before Panty left for Florida, he asked me to keep something for him. He said it was the only con-nection left with his old life, but that it was ter-ribly important "in case anything happened." It was a small envelope containing two flat keys to a safety-deposit box. Panty did not tell me what was in the box, but said that it had been rented for him by Stirnie Maize, but that Stirnie couldn't get into the box because he had surrendered both keys to Panty. I have no idea what any of this means, Doc, but please, please don't let it hurt us.
>   Grace Larkin.
>
> P.S. I've finally made up my mind to tell you where the keys are. They are in the little bronze vase on your mantel. I dropped them there while you were making me a drink. Please destroy this note.
>   G.

I crumpled up the note and shoved it into my trousers' pocket. Pay-off! Stirnie Maize, who said Burke was a bum, a double crosser and a rat! Stirnie Maize had rented a box for Burke and given Panty both keys. Now somebody wanted them back badly enough to beat Grace Larkin up and raid her room. I made up my mind then, for sure, that Burke was out of it entirely. If Burke had wanted the keys, he'd simply have asked for them. He may even have known where Grace Larkin kept them in her apartment, to which I suspect he had a key.

I went up to my room and carefully burned the letter in an ash tray and flushed the ashes down the john. I called up the New Haven and found I could get a train at five-thirty, a fast but milk job. Something told me that I was on the homestretch and that Eddie Marsh was still wallowing in a lot of badly assorted facts.

Too many facts, that was it. Too many unrelated things going on between too few people. Somewhere there was a small key, maybe even the keys on my mantel, that would unlock the whole thing and make it simple. I had the feeling that it had been the rest of us who had complicated the relationships. There was nothing very complex about people like Stirnie Maize, or Midge Manson, or even Burke. People like that—people who hide out in places and print phony mutuel tickets—don't usually turn out to be so smart when the law catches up with them. This thing had to be simple. I got very enthusiastic about the safety-deposit box.

At four-thirty I made up my mind it was worth a couple of days' hotel bill to annoy Eddie Marsh and I went out without my bags. I found an all-night restaurant and had breakfast. There was a morning paper on the back bar and I asked for it, mulling over the sports pages as I drank three cups of coffee. Before I left, I went back to the can and while I was washing my hands I absently looked out the window. There was an alley out there and a pretty bright light at the back of the building. I was about to turn away when I caught a glimpse of a guy coming around the corner into the alley. He stopped and backed into the shadows. It was the big cop who had visited Eddie. That's why he called when I arrived at the hotel.

I decided to try to lose him. If he was dumb enough to let me see him from the washroom window I might be able to get away with it. My breakfast had been paid for, the counterman

had left the check and I had put down the money without bothering to go to the cashier. I could leave any way I wanted. There
was a back door I'd noticed in the hall beyond the can entrance.
The cop had to be watching both that and the front. He had
come back to the alley because he didn't want me out that back
door. He had to come all the way around the corner to do it.
The thing to do was to send him back to the front again.

I wiped my hands carefully and started out the door of the
lavatory. Then, as if remembering, I came back and turned out
the light. I walked directly out the back door and down the
alley away from where the guy had been standing. I had a bad
moment until I got to the side street and into another alley. The
guy had seen me leave the washroom and had dutifully beaten
it back to the front door.

I got on the five-thirty without running into him any more.
I was right up to the pay-off, and I knew it.

16

I called Katie and made a date for New Year's Eve. Then I set out to find Stirnie Maize. The keys had lain, dusty and undisturbed, at the bottom of my little brass vase and I had them on my ring. I had no idea what I was running into but I figured I wouldn't have any trouble with Stirnie on the street or in a public place. I didn't think much of him as a tough guy anyway.

I tried up and down Jacobs Beach and a couple of bars without any luck. Finally, toward one o'clock, I caught up with him in the Eighth Avenue place where he eats chile. He was still sitting there with a handful of crackers, as if he hadn't moved since I'd seen him last.

"Hello, Stirnie." He looked up and wasn't happy about it. He made use of a mouthful of chile to stall me, nodded his head toward the seat opposite. I sat down.

"Hello, Doc. What do you know?"

"Not a hell of a lot, Stirnie." He went on eating, head down. "I'm still trying to help your friend Grace Larkin out of her trouble."

"Yeah? You gettin' any place?"

"Not too far. I've learned some things. How's the chile?"

"Usually pretty good here. I like it."

I flagged down the waiter and ordered some. "Yeah, Stirnie, I've gotten hold of some stuff that may help."

Maize looked out over the room. "Help what, Doc?"

"Mostly . . ." I decided it was time to shove the guy around a little, "Mostly to help me catch up with the louse who mauled Grace Larkin and tore up her room looking for something."

"Yeah . . . but . . ."

"Stow it a minute, Stirnie!" I ground it out, tough. "I'm looking for the guy who did that and who called her up the night Peters was killed and scared her out of her apartment . . ."

"But what could . . ."

"Shut up! I'm sore and I mean business. You can talk when I get through. You can talk, plenty."

The waiter came with my chile. I paid for it and he went away. "I'm looking for the guy who, all along, has known too much about everybody in this case—everybody." I let that sink in. "It's all the same guy, Stirnie, it's all the same guy and I think it's you."

This time he looked up—bewildered might be the word for it. He looked bewildered and sick. He put his spoon down. His hands shook like a drunk's. His voice was hoarse with something or other, complicated by startled and unswallowed chile.

"But it isn't me, Doc. It isn't me. I didn't have no part of any of it."

"Okay, Stirnie. So you didn't have any part of it." I took hold of his wrist. "Listen! I've been trying to do this thing without the cops so far, but I'll tell you one thing. If you don't talk straight to me about this business—about what you know about this business—I'm damned well going to turn you over to them and let them beat it out of you."

"The cops have got nothing on me." Scared. Scared and sullen.

"By God, they will have when I get through. I can throw you right into the middle of this case and you know it, at least you know somebody can. That somebody's me, Stirnie."

"But honest, Doc . . ."

"That somebody's me, Stirnie. There are things I want to know that you don't want me to know, that you don't want anybody to know. You're going to tell me those things or you're going to have one hell of a time explaining to Eddie Marsh why you were tangled up with Panty Burke."

"I was never tangled up with Burke. I told you what I thought of him. Burke and I never did no business."

"Maybe not. Maybe only once."

"What do you mean, only once?"

"You did Burke a favor once, didn't you?"

"What kind of a favor?"

"Don't stall. I asked you a question. *Did* you do Burke a favor at one time?"

"Why, I . . ."

"Okay, Maize, I'll answer it for you. You rented a safety-deposit box for Burke, didn't you?"

"Yes." He looked like your Aunt Jessie on a rough crossing.

"Tell me about it."

"All right, I will. I've got nothing to lose." To my disappointment, he brightened up considerably. I had the feeling, I was losing another suspect by the minute. Stirnie leaned across the table and spoke earnestly. "Burke came to me just before he left for Florida, just before he disappeared. He said he had some papers to put in a safe place and that he didn't want to leave them in his own name and he couldn't carry them with him. I was to rent the box and turn the keys over to him—that is after we had gone down together and left the stuff."

"And you did that?"

"Yes. I rented the box one day and we went down to the bank the next morning. I gave him the keys and he gave me a hundred dollars."

"That was all that happened?"

"That was all. I never saw him again."

"Did you ever see, or did Burke ever tell you what the papers were?"

"No."

"What did they look like? You had to be with him or he couldn't have gotten in."

"I only saw a single envelope, an ordinary long one like you can buy any place, no printing."

"Was it thick or thin? I mean did it look like it should have a rubber band around it, or did it look like a letter?"

"It was thin like a letter, only no address or anything."

I ate some chile and did some thinking. It couldn't have been bookmaking records. They'd been found where Peters was killed anyway. Thin like a letter. I got the exciting thought that it was probably a statement . . . a . . . what? Confession? Evidence against enemies? It had to be something like that. And, if it was something like that, I probably was at the windup. It didn't occur to me at the moment whose windup it was going to be. I also wondered who else might know of the safety-deposit-box deal. Stirnie was in a deep study. He jumped when I spoke.

"I want to see that envelope."

"Godamighty, Doc. I couldn't do that."

"Why? You can put it back just as it was."

"But Burke . . . there's Burke to think about . . ."

"I'll say there is. And I'm thinking about him. Look here, Stirnie. I'm going to take you at your word. For the moment, I'm going to believe that you're telling the truth—that you didn't break into Grace Larkin's place looking for those keys to cover yourself up. But *somebody* did, Stirnie, somebody who won't stop at anything to get them. Right?"

"I suppose so, Doc."

"Okay, then. Who would know about the deal you made with Burke over the box?"

"No one, no one that I'd know about." He looked sick again. "I see what you mean. I could . . . I . . ."

"That's right. You could be the next to go, fella. From the time the news gets out that the envelope can't be recovered without you, you're going to be . . . persuaded."

"Yeah." He looked down the bar where there were a lot of guys standing. "Yeah. A guy who'd beat a woman up like that . . ."

"You've got the idea. Shall we look at the envelope—just go down to the bank and see what this mug wants out of circulation so badly? Then we'll put it back neatly and blow. What do you say?"

"You don't think we should get the cops to go along?" The idea was intensely distasteful to the little guy, but he had only distasteful ideas to choose from at the moment.

"Why? It's your box. You rented it and paid for it. The bank has no interest in your visit so long as you sign the book and behave yourself. Plenty of time for the cops when you have to have them. The envelope will still be there."

"Maybe you're right, Doc. I wouldn't trust a lot of people in a spot like this but I know you'll do the right thing. You won't tell the cops until you have to, though, will you?"

"I won't tell the cops at all unless it has some direct bearing on the Peters murder, or Burke's criminal activities, if any."

"It's a deal, then. Maybe you can take some of the pressure off."

"If the envelope is what I think it may be, I can take a lot of the pressure off. Off both Larkin and you. Let's go. We've got time."

The bank was the Phillips Trust, or a branch of it on West Forty-sixth. I piled Maize into a cab before he lost his nerve and we were off. The whole process at the bank was very simple. Stirnie took the long, flat box and went into a little booth. I stood behind him as he opened the envelope. There was a smaller envelope inside on which writing appeared. Stirnie said: "Say, Doc . . ." and handed it to me. It read:

> The contents of this envelope were therein sealed by me, Joseph J. McGarrity, Notary Public, in the presence of William Edward Burke and Parker L. Manson and by their request.

The date followed and the signature of all three. The envelope had been sealed on September twenty-fourth with a glob of sealing wax and the notarial stamp imprinted into both wax and paper.

I said, "This changes the picture, Stirnie. We'll have to take it to a notary."

"Why? I don't like that much."

"Simple enough. The way the envelope stands, it's evidence, admissible evidence, of whatever it contains. It proves that both Panty Burke and Pike Manson agreed to sealing the thing up. If it's been tampered with, it loses its authenticity. It could have been changed or something else substituted. If we open it in the presence of another notary and he watches us, then seals it up again, it is still, theoretically at least, untouched."

"I don't quite get it, Doc, but I've gone this far and I guess there ain't any use in welchin' now."

There was a notary in the Safety Deposit Department and I explained to her that we wished to examine the contents of the letter together but, for purposes of legal good faith with the original signators of the letter, we wished her to witness the process to make certain there were no alterations or additions made during the period. She seemed bored and said that the process was not unusual, that it was employed once in a while in the examination of trust documents and other private papers.

She, herself, at our direction, opened the envelope and handed me the enclosure. Stirnie read over my shoulder. The letter had been written the same day it had been notarized. It read:

> TO WHOM IT MAY CONCERN!
> For the sum of five thousand dollars ($5000) and other considerations, I, Parker L. Manson, do release my former partner, William Edward Burke, from any obligation whatever, financial or otherwise, which may have been mutually incurred during our partnership.
>
> I, further, state that this dissolution of the aforementioned partnership was brought about, at the insistence of the above William Edward Burke, due to his unwillingness to participate in certain activities and associations into which I am about to enter. It is the intention and purpose of this statement to point out this unwillingness and consequent dissociation.
>
> Parker L. Manson.

The statement was witnessed by Burke and, in itself, not notarized. The notary had probably not read the statement itself. Most likely, a busy notary could have completely forgotten the whole transaction—or, at least, never associated it with

Panty Burke's disappearance. There are a lot of Burkes. Manson's name had had very little mention in the Burke stories and nothing at all had been made of his uninteresting death.

I folded up the paper and handed it to the woman who sealed it in a new envelope while we figured out what to say on it. As we put the thing back in the box and left the bank, I had a hell of a letdown feeling. Somehow, Burke's attempt to deal himself out of Manson's future, and undoubtedly criminal, activities didn't add much to what I'd already been going on. But it did blow a hell of a hole in the theory that Burke had stolen Pike Manson's dough.

We walked uptown again and Stirnie didn't have much to say. What he did have to say could be rolled into the statement, "Well, Doc, maybe Burke wasn't such a heel after all." I said maybe he wasn't and left Stirnie at the corner of Forty-eighth.

At least the paper proved one thing, or had a tendency to prove it, and that was that Panty Burke was trying to get away clean. It didn't prove, however, that he had done it. I was a little slow getting around to the main point.

Who the hell wanted that piece of paper so badly? And why? It had to be Midge Manson. That would be it. Some of the counterfeit mutuel tickets had turned up after Pike Manson's death. It might have been Peters who made and passed them, and it might have been somebody Midge had picked up to work with her. Who would have killed Peters if Peters, himself, had been making the phonies? Midge Manson could have. She'd been in town. Then the other guy she'd tied up with, Maximilian again, could have done the other stuff like raiding Larkin.

Plugging along that way, I got home and went up to the apartment. There was still time to catch the Merchants to Boston and I decided I'd better get back there.

There was nothing much in the mail and Katie's phone didn't answer at home although she'd left the office immediately after her show. Then the phone rang. It was the Boston operator: "Dr. Connor?" I asked who was calling Dr. Connor. "Boston is calling."

"The Doctor is at his office at the moment. Who's calling from Boston?"

"Just a minute." Mumbo-jummery. "Miss Larkin is calling Dr. Connor. Is he there?"

"Yes. This is he. Put her on." Clanging of quarters.

"Doc. I've got to make this fast. I'm at the phone in the ladies' room off the lobby. Marsh is outside waiting for me and losing his mind."

"What's the matter with . . ."

"Don't you talk. Let me. Listen. He's sending the cops for you—to your apartment. I heard him give the orders a couple of minutes ago. He's raving mad. Get out of your apartment and stay there. Call me at my room in fifteen minutes, five-eleven. If Marsh is there I'll stall. Be sure to call me and get away from your place. I've got a lot to tell you. 'By."

She hung up and I grabbed my hat and coat and jumped for the elevator. It was on my floor as I'd left it and I pressed the basement button. I could have memorized the *Iliad* while it went down. Jake Koff, the janitor, was there and I told him a cop would be around that I didn't want to talk to, to tell the cop I was in Boston. The old guy never questioned the instructions and I dove up the alley steps and out into Forty-eighth. No police car yet. A cab was passing and I jumped into that. Grace's fifteen minutes were almost up when we pulled up on the Lexington Avenue side of Grand Central. I ducked by the ticket window and got a quick one-way to Boston and beat it for the telephone office almost directly across the way. The cops would have to go back to Headquarters and report to Eddie that I wasn't there before they'd start looking for me at Grand Central.

I called room five-eleven at the Copley and Grace answered. I asked her if it was okay and she said yes.

"I stuffed pillows around the bell box. They can't have heard the bell even if their door is open."

"They? Are there more besides Marsh?"

"There are a dozen of them. They've been milling around all day. Marsh is furious with you. He thinks you've gummed the entire works."

"Oh-oh! Tell me about it."

"Well, Marsh and a Boston detective took me out to see Midge Manson today, a little before noon. They had said at her job that she'd reported she was ill. We got there and she'd cleared out."

"When had she left?"

"The landlady said she'd been gone about an hour when we got there."

"Why's Marsh so sore at me. I didn't send her away."

"He thinks you did, he says he knows you did."

"That's silly. How?"

"After we'd been to Midge Manson's rooming house, they took me down the street a couple of blocks to a saloon . . ."

"Oh-oh! That *isn't* so silly!"

"The man there didn't want to talk much but when Marsh told him you weren't any kind of a detective at all, the guy gave up and said you'd been there with Midge last night, that you'd been in a fight or something and that she'd fixed up your head."

"Oh, brother!"

"It was true, then?"

"Yes. I got slugged by her boy friend, probably the guy who beat you up. I didn't see who it was. What happened after that?"

"That was when Marsh got so mad. As soon as he got back to the hotel, he started telephoning New York. He threatened to all the way back."

"All right, Grace. Thanks for warning me. You'll hear from me soon. How long does Marsh plan to keep you there?"

"Indefinitely. He's got some reason to believe Panty Burke is in Boston and he's keeping me under—how do they term it?—protective surveillance until he catches him. It's pretty awful, Doc. I keep wondering . . ."

"Don't keep wondering. I'll get in touch with you very soon. There in Boston. Maybe tomorrow. Keep your chin up. So long."

I hid in the welcome dark of the newsreel theater until it was time to catch the Merchants at five.

17

I climbed off the train at Back Bay wondering where to head. It was a cinch that the Midge Manson neighborhood would be lousy with cops and I couldn't look for much help from Pat the bartender now that Eddie had washed me up there. That's why I hadn't ridden on into South Station.

I walked over to the Copley and went in as casually as I could. The usual, good-looking evening crowd was around and there were quite a few people to help me look inconspicuous. But, before I got to the elevator, I learned I hadn't been over-looked. A huge blue suit, complete with big, black shoes and a guy, stopped me. A new one this time.

"You Doc Connor?"

I said, "Okay, sergeant. Eddie Marsh wants to see me?"

"Yeah. Plenty." He didn't smile any when he said it. "We'll go up to room five-ten."

We did. Without conversation and in the spirit of good fellowship you find between a couple of Brahma bulls. The guy had been carefully taught not to like any part of me. He rapped on five-ten and Eddie hollered to come in. He was sitting at the little hotel desk writing something. He looked up and started to say something. It was not going to be nice. Then he put his pen down, very carefully.

"Thanks, Davis. You can report back." Davis went out and closed the door. Marsh looked at me for some time. "Well, Doc, you got in my way once too often."

"How?"

"That isn't what I tell you, my smart friend, that's what you tell me. You're going to tell me a lot of things, chum, and then you're going to get out of this business, and stay out. Now start talking."

"I may have something for you, but I'm damned if I'm taking a lot of crap like that, from you or anybody else. If you've got anything to arrest me for, go ahead and throw me in the can. If you haven't, turn me loose and call off those mugs you've got tailing me around."

"If what you've got for me is about where Panty Burke is holed up, or how I can find out . . ."

"It isn't." I wanted to leave it there but I couldn't after I saw the expression on the big ape's face. "Or, at least, I don't think it is."

"Who hit you over the head?"

"Probably the guy who killed Ernie Peters." I let him have it easy like, casual.

"Don't be so goddam smart! I'm not having any. How'd you run into Burke?"

"I don't think it was Burke. I don't think any of this is Burke."

"All right, all *right!* What you think is of no interest to me at all. I want to know what happened, and why Midge Manson was fixing up your head in a barroom."

"You get around, don't you!"

"*I* get around!" The guy was really fuming. "I get around! Listen! Every damned place I've gone for the last three days, you've just left—and not only that, but you've scared my witnesses off at the same time. Let's have it, Doc."

I told him about the night I had followed Midge Manson through the alley and what happened, later, in the bar. He didn't say anything. I left out my visit with Stirnie Maize, thought I'd hold it out for trading purposes. It's uncomfortable as hell to be on that kind of a basis with your best friend and I hoped maybe I could placate Eddie with a few handy bits of information. When I wound up, he said:

"Why did you come up here in the first place?"

"Because I believed Grace Larkin's story. Why are you here, yourself, Eddie?"

"What story?"

"All of it." For emphasis, I projected—as Katie would call it. Maybe I barked.

"Don't holler at me. I got about all I can take." He picked up his fountain pen and threw it down again. "Why would believing Larkin bring you up here? She tell you anything I don't know?"

"I don't know what she told you, and it doesn't make much difference. I believed her when she said that Panty Burke wasn't kidding her about being pretty well in the clear before the day he started for Florida. If that's the case, nothing about the whole affair—as you, the police, understand it—makes any sense."

Eddie rubbed his hand through his hair. He looked like hell. He looked too tired to be very sore at anybody very much longer. "Nothing about it makes any sense anyway. We're right back where we started. The man, Burke, is a wraith. He disappears right in front of thousands of people at Penn Station; he hangs around New York and kills a guy with whom he's supposed to be in a counterfeiting deal; he beats up his girl and tears up her place looking for something; he steals groceries in a rented truck; and the best police force in the world can't lay a hand on him."

"But if you were looking for the wrong guy . . ."

"Oh, please, Doc, don't give me that again. It's a hell of a fine sentimental idea, sponsored by a beautiful gal. That's all right for you—but you haven't got any evidence. They'd laugh me out of the office. It won't work."

"I've got more, Eddie."

"More? What?"

"I can prove that Panty Burke paid Manson off for the partnership before he left, or tried to leave, for Florida."

"*What!*"

"What's more, I can prove that Burke went on record as breaking up the partnership because Manson intended to go into a deal Burke didn't like."

"By Grace Larkin's story, of course. It isn't worth a dime, Doc. We know everything she has."

"Grace Larkin doesn't know a thing about it. That statement is sealed up and put away in a safety-deposit box, sworn to and dated by a notary."

"How do you know?"

"I saw it." The man opened his mouth. Closed it.

"Listen, Eddie. There's only one thing, one single thing that Grace Larkin knew that she didn't tell you. Know what that was?"

"Let's not play games. You know how much this means to me, Doc."

I was sorry for the mug but I had to make some sort of a deal for the Larkin hide. "I wasn't playing games. Grace Larkin *thought* she had her lover's destiny in her hands, her last possible service to him, the care of two keys, two, flat safety-deposit keys . . ."

"Then she knew all along what . . ."

"Yes. She knew what the man was after when he slugged her. She had no idea what was in the box, but she *did* know—and she's always known—that it wouldn't have been Burke who beat her up trying to get them."

"But Burke couldn't have had a box. We check that sort of thing as a part of routine in cases like this."

"The box was in Stirnie Maize's name."

"Maize! That little . . . the rat who gave you the original tips on Burke and on Larkin?"

"That's right. The fellow who knew that Midge Manson had been in New York the day Peters was killed."

Eddie thought this over for a moment, then glowered at me for the first time in several minutes. "Doc, how long have you known this?"

"Seven or eight hours." I guess I grinned because he grinned back.

"Tell me about it."

"I'll not only tell you about it, but I'll turn the keys over to you without question—if you'll not ask me where I got them until you've wound up the case."

"Where did I get them, then?"

"They had been hidden in Larkin's apartment. Won't that do in the report?"

"I suppose so." He practiced on the words a while, then, "Yes, I guess that'll do. Now. Gimme the keys and tell me about it." I hauled the things out of my wallet and handed them to Eddie. Then I told him the story of my visit to Stirnie, our trip to the notary's and the bank. I repeated, as well as I could remember, the text of the agreement.

For the next ten minutes Eddie was on the phone with the office. I felt a fleeting twinge of something or other about Stirnie. I hardly envied him his evening.

When Marsh sat back and looked at me again, he seemed considerably calmer—hardly friendly but not actively hostile. "Know any more to tell me?"

"Yes."

"Good, Lord! What?"

"Whoever hit me over the head the other night needed some Packard manifold gaskets.

"Packard gaskets! There's no car in this deal any place."

"1939 Packard manifold gaskets." I told him of following Midge while she shopped, and of the prearranged call at the drugstore pay booth. That sent him to the telephone again, this time to the Boston police.

"I wish you'd told me that sooner, Doc."

"We weren't on speaking terms."

"All right, all right—but the woman is gone. Probably in that 1939 Packard." He opened and closed that helpless black notebook of his and frowned at the wastebasket—for all the world like he'd have enjoyed chucking the thing into it. "All this doesn't add a damned thing. It's just so much confusing trash lying around which doesn't seem to belong to the main issue. I got to find Burke."

"He won't be in that 1939 Packard."

"Why not? Because he wouldn't be with the Manson gal?"

"Yes. He'd be as far away from her as he could get."

"I suppose so. She pretended to hate his guts."

"She did hate his guts. What's more, if your theory is right and Burke is running around loose someplace, Midge Manson is running away from him, not with him."

"With a pocketful of Packard manifold gaskets?"

"With a guy who knows how to use them when he needs to."

"It could be innocent enough, couldn't it?"

"I suppose it could. From what I've seen of the Manson woman, she hasn't performed an innocent act since she wet her first diaper."

"She's nobody's bargain." Eddie hoisted up to his feet and looked down at me. "Listen, Doc. I never knew a guy in my life who could burn me up like you do. You're bull-headed and wilful and you haven't got the brains of an ostrich . . ."

"Hey! Wait a minute! Here I . . ."

"I know, I know . . . I . . ."

"I know a story about a guy who always said I know, I know."

"Quiet. I'll be off my chump any minute. I want to get some sleep and I want to think and I damned well want to be alone—as soon as I get one thing off my chest."

"Okay. Shoot. Never mind the prologue this time."

"I'm thankful to you for this information. I haven't the slightest idea what I'm going to do with it, but I suppose it'll come in handy when I get Burke and I thank you for it. Now." His tremendous fists opened and shut. "Now, will you please, for the love of all that's holy, go *home* and fix some horse's leg or something?"

"Sure. Sure I will. I'll go away tomorrow." Eddie eyed me with some suspicion.

"I don't like the way you said that. It was dirty."

"How you talk, Loot. I've given you my promise. I'll leave Boston sometime tomorrow . . . what'd you want me to do? Take that damned milk train again?"

"I can think of worse ideas. What you want to do in the meantime? Got something on your mind?"

"Yeah. A hell of an idea."

"What?"

"Take Grace Larkin dancing downstairs. There's an hour or so left and she's in need of some cheering up." It was a quickie but got better as I thought it over.

"Why . . . that's no good . . ."

"With all those cops you've got posted down there?"

"I haven't got any cops down there."

"False! If that little dried-up guy with the bald head and the newspaper upside-down isn't a cop . . ."

"So I've got one. I forgot the guy. Tell him to call me when you go down. I'll send him home. It's silly but I guess it's all right. Go ahead. I'll tell Katie, though, you know."

"Yes. I know. 'Night, matie."

"Good night . . . you clown!"

18

I had asked Grace, as we sat in the big, gay room, if she knew what Burke had left in Stirnie Maize's box. She had listened a while to the music, good music, an old friend's, Rannie Weeks'.

"You see, Doc, that was the trouble. I was afraid he'd buried things in that box that might hurt him, maybe the last of his old life. No. I didn't know what was in the box. He didn't want me to know, apparently."

I told her what I'd discovered. She had had tears in her eyes when she'd said, "He did want everything straight, didn't he!"

Now, rolling west on the B & M through the early morning, I thought a lot about how straight Panty Burke had wanted things. I thought about how nothing in the whole, nasty business belonged to a guy who wanted things straight. What could have happened to Burke that would have justified his disappearance, his absence of weeks—then his reappearance in New York on some mission of vengeance. It had to be something like that because Eddie and his fingerprint boys had placed him at the scene of Peters' killing. The hazy figure of Maximilian Wardhouse floated again in my mulling. I felt more and more certain that Max, whoever he was, had come into the picture and distorted it until straight-thinking people couldn't follow the strange, unrelated happenings.

Did I say I was going west on the B & M? That isn't toward New York. That's toward Middle Fairfield where Pike Manson had been found dead. It was only a vague hunch, but it was an angle which had apparently gone uninvestigated. Uninvestigated, at least, since it had, weeks ago, been dismissed as having no bearing on the major issues.

It seemed to me that if Pike Manson had, somehow, been murdered, a lot of the ill-assorted facts of the case would fall into place. I don't know why I had guts enough to start out to discover that when police of both Middle Fairfield and from New York had already accepted his death as natural, or at least as natural as acute alcoholism ever is.

But the idea kept recurring. Give me the murder of Manson by, let's say, Maximilian Wardhouse, and I'll show you some reason for all of the screwy things we couldn't otherwise fit together.

Maximilian knows that Manson and Peters have cooked up a successful way to beat the mutuel-ticket counterfeiting racket. Maybe it was his process in the first place and one of them took it away from him. Maybe he was being blackmailed by one of them. Maybe he was, in some way, blackmailing them—or Burke.

Don't get the idea that Max couldn't have been Burke. Certainly all Eddie Marsh's evidence bore that out in a straight line. But then Eddie didn't have Maximilian to work with. He didn't have anybody but Burke.

So Max cooks up a way to kill Manson, then, as I figure it, offers a deal to Peters, which Peters accepts. (The phony tickets appeared during that interval . . . or started to appear.) Then I scare Peters and he runs to Maximilian and loses his nerve. Max shoots him and walks out. Because he is Max, and not anybody the police are looking for, his job of hiding out is simplified. Right?

What about Burke? From the time Max kills Manson, Burke doesn't dare show his face. His whole plan, through no fault of his own, has blown up right in front of him. The one thing that must not happen is that Grace Larkin be involved. Give that to Burke and his disappearance is simple.

Yes, I can make sense—maybe not the motives I've guessed but something equally simple—I can make sense out of the whole thing, given the murder of Pike Manson.

I fought off thinking about ways in which it could have been done. I needed to stick to facts from here in—and, besides, they weren't convincing.

I checked my bag at the station and asked where the local police headquarters was. I walked the five blocks through sun on snow. Middle Fairfield is one of those substantial New England manufacturing towns that you'd recognize if you found one in Africa.

The desk sergeant said that the Chief was over at the Courthouse and what did I want?

"I'm interested in learning some facts in connection with the death of a man named Parker Manson, Parker L. Manson."

"Why?" Just like that. I figured the Chief might make it tough for me, but this guy caught me a little off base.

"I have been helping the New York Police in connection with a matter we believe may be tied up with this."

"Are you a police officer?"

"No. I'm a physician. My name is James Connor."

"Have you a letter to us?"

"As a matter of fact I haven't. I came here on a sudden notion, an idea based on things I'd discovered in Boston, with Lieutenant Marsh of the New York Department."

"Lieutenant Marsh. Yes. We've had a visit from him. Some weeks ago." The sergeant answered the phone, mumbled a few words of cop-ese and hung up.

"I'll tell you, Doctor, Chief Bradley will be back in a few minutes. He just went up there to testify in a d&d which shouldn't take long. Would you like to wait?"

"Sure. Thanks."

"Sit down over there." He pointed to a bench near the desk and I sat. "I guess you know I couldn't give you any files without the boss said so."

"Of course, Sergeant. I don't suppose the Chief will, either, unless I can identify myself pretty well with him."

"He's a careful fella and a good chief of police. He's held the job through a good many changes in town politics."

"That's saying a lot nowadays. How long's he been chief?"

"I think it's sixteen years. . . . Yes. We gave him a big blow-out on his fifteenth anniversary last June."

The phone rang again and I lit a cigarette. A sick-looking guy came from the back someplace and went dazedly out into the sunshine. He had civilian clothes and an Army overcoat. A big, oldish man passed him at the door and they both stopped.

"Done it out, Jack?"

"Yeah. I done it out, Chief. All but six days."

"I hope they give you Northampton next time. They'll help you up there. So long, Jack."

"So long, Chief."

The big man walked through the corridor and glanced at me as he reached for the swinging panel next to the desk sergeant. The sergeant mumbled to him and he turned.

"You waitin' for me?"

"Yes, Chief."

"Come in back." He led the way to his big old-fashioned office. Dust, books, sunshine and a rubber plant. I sat in a massive, worn leather chair and told him just about what I'd told the sergeant. He hauled out a cigar, looked at it and looked at me as though perplexed. A nice guy. I told him I preferred cigarettes although he hadn't offered the cigar. He gave me a glance of approval.

"You say you've been working with Marsh?"

"Yes. Unofficially, you understand. We've had some experiences before in which I've been able to dig up little things for him. Eddie Marsh is my best friend."

"Seems like a fine feller, little I saw of him." The Chief took a penknife from the desk and carefully cut off the end of his cigar. "I'll tell you, Doctor, under ordinary circumstances I'd feel perfectly free to give you anything you want here. On the other hand, in view of the interest of the New York Police Department—or, at least the interest they showed some weeks ago in the Manson file—I think I should call up Marsh. You say he's in Boston?"

I crossed my fingers and squirmed as I gave him the number and he relayed it to the desk sergeant. I thought I'd better pave the way for the explosion.

"Eddie will probably be sore as a goat with me for digging into this end of the thing. He doesn't think there's anything here."

"What sort of thing? What sort of thing would you expect to find here?"

"I'm not quite sure, Chief, but I do know that, if Manson *could*, under any possible circumstances, have been murdered, the whole case would fall into line . . . which it doesn't now."

"You say the whole case. Do you mean the Burke disappearance?"

"Yes. And the killing of a man named Ernest Peters."

"I see. Well I'm afraid you've run into a blind switch here. Manson wasn't murdered." He puffed his cigar complacently. "It's all in the file."

"I suppose so. I thought it wouldn't hurt to review it. As a doctor, you see . . ."

"We think Doc Parsons is about as good as they come and he didn't find anything."

The phone rang and I had a moment of wishing I'd gone on home to New York. The Chief hollered hello, hello and I heard the receiver buzzing with the rasp of Eddie's bass.

"There's a feller in my office that wants access to the file on Parker Manson, the case you was here asking . . ."

The receiver went to work again and, after a while, the Chief looked strangely at me, his bushy old eyebrows raised distinctly.

"Yes. That's who he is all right. He seems like a nice enough feller. Wait a minute, Lieutenant." The Chief put his hand over the transmitter and said, "He don't act like he thinks much of you, Doctor, want to talk to him?"

I picked up the phone and helloed Eddie.

"You promised me you'd go home and leave this thing alone."

"I said I'd leave Boston and I did. Listen, Eddie, this is just a hunch and can't do any harm . . ."

"Don't tell me how much harm you can do. I know. Besides, Doc, don't be an ass. We went over all that. What you trying to prove?"

"That Pike Manson didn't die a natural death. Think, Eddie, what that would do to the case if Manson could have been murdered!" There was a little silence and Eddie said to put the Chief on again. When the old fellow hung up, he grinned.

"You fellers must be pretty good friends."

"We are, usually. Why, Chief?"

"Because nobody would ever used such scurrilous statements about anybody but his best friend or his worst enemy." He dumped the ashes of his cigar partly in the ash tray, the rest on his vest. "Now. What do you want to know about the Parker Manson business?"

He went over to his filing cabinets and dug out a thin file, spread it on the desk before him.

"I'd like to know everything about it." The big fellow looked at me with a touch of genial fun around his eyes. He picked the top sheet and held it in front of him.

"I'm sure you would, Doctor. Wouldn't it come closer to the truth to say that you'd like to know something about it that we don't know?"

It wasn't a challenge. I didn't take it as such, somehow. I thought that here was a guy I could work with. He was fair enough not to take my inquiry defensively. "It's this way, Chief. I take it for granted that you and your men are as thorough as police everywhere have to be these days." He looked at the end of his cigar and said nothing. "I also take it for granted that your Medical Examiner . . ."

"What's all this about, son?"

"Simply that the Parker Manson story may be a very simple one, cut and dried. But a lot of other facts, facts you haven't yet learned about people you don't yet know, make it look as though he *should* have been murdered." The old chap confined to sit in silence. "All I'm saying is that if what had seemed to be a routine police matter could possibly have been a murder, all these other facts would lead us to the man who committed it, and at least one more."

"Well, I'll tell you. There's been a lot of homicides committed in this country that we haven't had anything to do with. But we've had a few during my years here and I think we've done

right ably with them. On the other hand, neither my Department
nor Doc Parsons is error-proof and if the worst we turn up is
a mistake, I'll stand on our record and not take it too hard."

"That's really encouraging. I didn't expect such a friendly
reception. What say you tell me about it?"

The Chief settled back in his chair and put on his glasses.
"On the morning of October nineteenth, a man named Wiczek,
a section hand on the Boston & Maine Railroad, reported a
body lying at the bottom of the railroad embankment at the
foot of Narbonne Street . . . it's an almost deserted section and
Narbonne dead-ends there . . ."

"But it can be reached by car?"

"Not easily . . . but it's possible." He lit his cigar again. "We
sent officers Kalt and Bassett to the scene. There they found
Manson . . ."

"How was he identified?"

"Not only by his wallet and a letter in his pocket, but, as a
matter of fact, we'd already been looking for him."

"Oh?"

"Some days previous to this, we had received a letter. Wait."
He shuffled in the file. "Here it is. You can read it for yourself."

It was dated October 15th and was on plain notepaper, the
envelope postmarked Boston. It read:

> Police Department,
>   Middle Fairfield, Massachusetts.
> Dear sir:
> My husband disappeared from his home in Boston
> some time ago while he was drunk. He is a habit-
> ual drunkard. The last I heard from him was from
> Middle Fairfield when he wrote for money to come
> home. I sent him twenty dollars hoping he would
> get back but I have not heard from him . . .

A rather detailed, though general, description followed and
several articles of clothing mentioned specifically. Also some of

the articles likely to be found in his wallet, including a picture of Midge. The letter was signed, Margaret Manson. The address was not the one on Wickland Street.

As I looked up the Chief said, "You see why we didn't hesitate too long on the identification."

"Certainly. This would do it . . . and this letter fits well with the rest of the facts. Manson had been leaving home, I'm told, on spasmodic drunks for weeks."

The big man at the desk went on. "The man had evidently been dead for some time, according to Parsons around twenty-four hours. The place had obviously been used by him for some time before that. There was the remains of a fire and an empty whisky bottle.

"What was in his stomach?"

"What would you expect? Alcohol." He looked back at the paper. "Doc Parsons has got a lot of doofaddle here. You can talk to him later. I'll just tell you my part."

"Right. Go ahead."

"In his pocket was a letter from his wife, same handwriting as the one you saw. You can look it over after I've gone to dinner. I'm speaking at, the Business Men's Association of Greater Fairfield. Anyway the letter is addressed Parker Manson, General Delivery here, was called for by a guy with booze on his breath, the clerk says, and it said, in effect, that here's a twenty and please be a good boy and come home." The Chief gave me a big grin. "That wraps it up pretty good, doesn't it?"

"It sure does. Then what?"

"Then we wired the woman that we'd found her husband and sent the body up to the hospital. We got sort of a morgue up there."

"You sent prints to Washington, of course."

"Of course, that's routine. As a matter of fact, Lieutenant Marsh already had copies of the prints from Washington when he came to see us about Manson. It was all very regular."

"I'm sure it was. Then Mrs. Manson arrived?"

"That's right. Mrs. Manson arrived with further identification of the body and herself—all very proper."

"What was the further identification of the body? Of her claim to it?"

The old chap beamed at me. "I never saw more positive identification. That's a smart woman, that Mrs. Manson."

"You aren't just kidding!" Brother! "What was the identification?"

"An x-ray picture of his chest! Doc says it showed some old rib fractures that couldn't be mistaken."

"You mean you opened the guy up again?"

"No. We just took another x-ray. Click, and we had the same picture—of the ribs, anyway. Positive."

"I'll say it's positive! So you let her take him."

"Of course. Why not? Dudley Small, the undertaker, took the body over and shipped it to a respectable undertaker in Boston. Mrs. Manson rode back as the escort."

"I'll bet she did! What about seeing Dr. Parsons?"

"Still want to see him?"

"I'm not too hopeful, but there might be something."

"Sure. There might. As I say, we're not mistake-proof, the Doc and I, but we been around a long time."

"There are just a couple of questions I'd like to ask him."

"His office is right in this block. Hadley Block the building's called. Fifth floor. He's all right, Doc is. He'll answer your questions. I'll call him up."

"That's kind of you. Thanks, Chief, I'm glad to have met you."

I wandered up the street to the Hadley Block, a dingy old brick building that had 1888 carved in one of the ornamental stones. Parsons was an elderly gent, stuffy as hell, and resentful from the start at what Chief Bradley had apparently told him over the telephone.

My conversation with the doctor was brief and lucid. He stated, without interruption, all the things I'd learned from the Chief and then told me he was busy. As I was being hustled out, I managed to ask him if there had been signs of any intravenous injection. He roared back at me in the face of an astonished waiting room full of Middle Fairfieldians.

"Hell, no! Don't you think I have the brains I was born with? There wasn't a mark on either ante cubital, nor a hypodermic mark any place on his body. He was murdered all right, young fellow, but his killer was a man by the name of John Barleycorn who kills a lot of my patients."

The guy looked around the room for a laugh and he got it. When he was through taking his bow, I asked, "Doctor. Had the man hurt his foot?"

"Why do you ask that? As a matter of fact he had, small abrasions. Nothing to pay any attention to."

"Did you include them in your report?"

"I can't remember. Why?" He'd caught my meaning and was defensive.

"Well, I suppose it isn't, but it could have been important."

I went back down to the first floor feeling pretty much as though I'd been wasting my time. I walked over to the hotel to get some lunch—dinner to all the locals. For some reason I ate a New England boiled dinner. For some other reason, I made up my mind to go back to Boston, Eddie or no.

19

I checked into a dump in Hartville Road, the possessor of a tremendous hunch. Julius, my friend of the Cecil, had philosophized that a hunch was the result of the unconscious organization of a lot of known facts. I hoped so, because it was a definite, well-organized conviction, demanding definite, well-organized action.

There were a lot of contributing factors to the hunch . . . and, after I got it, a lot of other factors fell into place. One was the abrasions on the dead Pike Manson's foot. One was the fact that a 1939 Packard made an excellent marine conversion for motorboats. One was the expert way Midge Manson dressed my head and her use of the word "sutures."

It was late in the afternoon when I started down Hartville Road toward the alley where I'd got slugged. I figured to take up the thing from there. If the gaskets were for a Packard marine conversion, an automobile engine rigged over for marine use, my guy Maximilian might have needed other parts. I walked the couple of short blocks to the waterfront streets and looked around for a boat-supply place. I ran into one immediately and went in. A salty looking young fellow with a limp waited on me.

"I've got hold of an old Packard engine and want to make a conversion for a cruiser hull I bought. Have you got the necessary parts?"

"Some. What I haven't got I can get for you." He slid his hip up on the counter as if he'd be willing to talk a while. "Takes time, though."

"I supposed it would. I'm going to do the work myself so I'll have plenty of time to wait for them. Anybody around here got a Packard conversion. I'd sure like to see how they're rigged."

"The fishin' boats have a lot of them. What model engine you got?"

"'39."

"I know a coupla fellas that's got '39 Packard conversions. One of them's out of town."

"I'd get a kick out of seeing one installed. They tell me they're okay if you get them bedded right."

"Yeah. They are. This other fella—I don't exactly know him. He come in for some stuff twice. I had some of it. I know he's got a '39 because of what he bought. Besides that he wanted special manifold gaskets and I didn't have 'em."

I could have bayed like a bloodhound. My hackles stood up a little at that. "Where does he keep his boat? You know?"

"No, I don't. But if he came here for the stuff he's likely tied up at the Tea Wharf. That's where the small ones go around here."

"I see. What sort of a looking guy? I might run across him down there."

"I dunno, fairly good size, kind of dark hair. He was pretty greasy when I seen him—like he'd been workin' on the engine just before. That's why I figured he's at the Tea Wharf."

"Yeah. That's right. I'll look him up. The fishermen may know him and his Packard conversion."

"Sure. You look around. If he comes in again, I'll tell him you're lookin' for him." The guy picked up a pencil and his sales pad. "Want to leave your name and phone number?"

I managed to muscle up a sort of a laugh while I was making up my mind and said, "Maybe he wouldn't call the police."

"I don't getcha, Mister."

I showed him my shoulder-holstered gun. He looked very much impressed and said, "Yeah?"

"Yeah." I offered him a cigarette and the chummery was on. "I might as well tell you, fella, that I haven't got a Packard engine and wouldn't know what to do with it if I had one."

"You're lookin' for clues, eh?"

"No. I got clues. I'm looking for the guy who tried to buy gaskets from you."

"What you want him for?"

"Can I trust you not to talk?"

"Sure. I'll help you if I can. What you want him for?"

I leaned over the counter and whispered, "Murder!"

". . . and that's the guy that done it? The guy was in here?"

"That's right. Now listen. You say you'll help. You also say the man's hands were greasy like he'd been working on the engine. Can you remember anything he handled while he was in here that hasn't been handled since?"

"Fingerprints?" He gave me a sickening leer. I told him he was right again, that he ought to be on the force.

"I've thought of it before this, Mister. I might be, but for my leg. Say, look. This man handled a lot of gaskets here, wrong sizes. Nice shiny metal surfaces. Want to look at 'em?"

"Yeah. Please. And be careful how you handle them. Get 'em by the edges."

"Right." He went to a shelf and pulled down a cardboard box. "This is the box. They would of fit his job and I told him so but he wanted the ones that were made for his engine."

One by one he put them out on the counter. "Mister, them gaskets have never been unpacked, never until he handled them. If they were wiped clean at the factory they can't have nobody's fingerprints on 'em except mine and the guy's."

We studied them over and, within the first half dozen, we found three with two clear sets of prints. On two, the prints were practically entire, only missing small portions which fell off the curve of the thin, flat plates. I asked him if he would mind giving me a set of his own prints for comparison.

"Hell, no. Uncle Sam's got 'em and, besides, I went down and left them once when they had a campaign for that. I believe in it."

"That's right. Good for you." He inked his fingers on his date stamp pad and gave me a nice set. I wrapped the gaskets carefully and shoved them in my pocket. The guy wouldn't take

anything for them because he said, that way, I would have to
come back and he wanted to find out what happened. I thanked
him and pulled out, promising to see him later.

There was a cab standing at the corner of Hartville Road and
I set off for the Copley. I kept thinking the same thought over
and over—no matter what has happened to confuse us before,
no matter what—I have, in my pocket, the fingerprints of the
guy who's in with Midge. I have in my pocket the fingerprints
of the guy who clouted me over the head. . . . I've got the prints
of Maximilian Wardhouse.

I tried to get five-ten on the house phone but Eddie must
have been out. I tried five-eleven and a man answered. I asked
for Grace Larkin and got her. She told me to come up and have
a drink. She had decided the detective Eddie had left in his
room was lonesome so she invited him in for a cocktail. Yes,
Eddie had flown to New York an hour or so ago but would be
back during the night. "Come on up."

She was sitting there with the big cop I'd seen going up to
Eddie's room the day before. She introduced him as Sergeant
Davis of the Boston police. Grace sent down for more martinis. The Sergeant seemed somewhat embarrassed and sat silent
while Grace and I exchanged some chatter, trying to figure out
how to talk in front of the guy. Finally I tossed a remark at him.

"Eddie go down to talk to Stirnie Maize, Sergeant?"

"You know about Maize?"

"Yeah. I brought that in for Marsh."

"Oh." He pondered a moment. "Yeah. The Lieutenant went
down to talk to Maize. They picked him up."

"I might have something more for him. Maybe not. It'll wait
until he gets back. You say he'll be back tonight?"

The cop frowned. "I sure hope so. I been on duty since seven
this morning. I got some work of my own to do, too."

"Too bad." I waited a while. "Say, Sergeant, is there an extra
set of all the prints in the Peters killing around somewhere?"

"Sure, Doc, they're all over the country. There's some in
the other room. Marsh brought up a bunch from New York, all
mounted on one sheet."

"Do you suppose you could spare me one?"

Davis laughed. "I don't know why not. Lieutenant Marsh was braggin' about you just last night while we was waiting around."

"Bragging? About me?"

"Yeah. You know how he is. He'd call you a lot of dirty names and then tell me how you worked out a case and damn near got yourself killed."

"I see. You don't suppose he'd mind, then, if I borrowed a set of those prints?"

The man got up and went to the door. "I'll get 'em myself."

He came back with the sheet and I folded it flat into my coat pocket. The waiter came with the martinis. I was burning to get away but had to stay a while, anyway. Conversation lagged. Finally Davis, who had finished his cocktail in one magnificent sweep, headed for the room across the hall.

"I guess you folks are old friends. I'll just go in the other room and finish my magazine. Thanks, lady, for the drinks."

Grace said come in again, Sergeant, and we were alone. I told her to talk and keep talking, to tell me some long tale while I did something important. She went right into the act . . .

"You know, Doc, that sort of a friendship is awfully strange. I suppose it happens only between men . . ." She went on and on as I hauled out the gaskets and took them into the bathroom. There was some fine-grained body powder on the shelf and I blew it over the strongly outlined mechanic's-grease prints. They showed plainly the first try and I blew it on again for luck. They stood out in clean relief.

I compared them with the sheet. One was strange—luckily the poorer one. The other was unmistakable. It matched exactly the print on the police sheet marked: "Left Thumb, William Edward Burke."

I could have bawled.

I stuck the whole damned works into the drawer of Grace Larkin's desk and sat down. She was still talking. I told her she could stop.

She said, "Did you do what you said was important, Doc?"

"Yes. I did."

"Was it important?" She smiled.

"Yes." How in God's dear name was I to do this? I'd learned to like this girl—to respect her and believe in the things she said—to believe with her, the things she believed. I had no choice. "It was as important as hell, Grace."

"To you?"

"To you. It was bad news, kid, end of the road news."

"Tell me."

"I've got to." I put my hand on hers and felt like a hypocritical heel because I was trying so hard to ease it off that I felt phony and self-conscious. "Look, Grace. It's Burke. It's been Burke all the way."

She didn't move a muscle. "Tell me."

"The rest of it's worse."

"Tell me, Doc."

"Burke is in town. In Boston. He's with Midge Manson." I watched the tension in her hands on the arms of her chair. I hesitated . . .

"Go on." She just said the two words but they were spring steel.

"He's got a boat down in the Bay somewhere and he's been fixing it up. Midge Manson has been helping him, buying supplies and stuff."

"You *know* this, Doc."

"Yes. I know it. I have a positive fingerprint on a piece of mechanical equipment he handled while he was shopping for parts. There's no doubt about it." She got up and walked across the room and back.

The explosion I was expecting didn't come. She just walked.

I said, "I'm sorry, Grace. . . . I wanted it so much to be our way."

"I know, Doc. You've been wonderfully kind."

She pulled up in front of me. "It's all right, Doc. I don't understand it, but I give up. These last weeks have done something to me that I can't quite understand, myself. I believe what you've told me tonight—just the facts—not the motives implied. Something terrible has happened to the Panty Burke I loved. Perhaps that something has also killed, in him, all the fine plans he'd made for himself, for us. I don't know. All I know is that whatever there had been in life for the two of us is spoiled. When he got no word to me for so long I was sure he must be dead. Then the telephone call the night Peters was killed. From what you've just told me, it must have been Midge Manson. I can't live with the picture of Panty Burke that's been painted by these things." She walked away again. "Now this!"

"I'm afraid you can forget him now, Grace."

"That's the hell of it. I can't forget him. I can forget I love him but I can't help thinking about him. A boat! A boat of all places to hide—wetness all around. Mid-winter in a boat! Oh, God, Doc! The poor bastard's got *tuberculosis!*"

"He's got what?"

"Tuberculosis—not too badly. He had a good chance before all this. That's why we were going into that lousy little business in Florida—he would have gotten well, Doc—the x-rays hardly showed anything . . ."

"What x-rays? Tell me quick!"

"Before he asked me to marry him he had x-rays made of his chest . . ."

"Where were those x-rays—never mind his condition for a minute—where were those x-rays?"

"Why Panty was taking them to the doctor in Florida. The New York doctor had . . . wait, Doc, what is it?"

I hollered to Davis on my way out and told him to keep an eye on Grace and that I'd get in touch with Eddie before the night was over.

20

I hopped a cab for Hartville Road and got out a couple of blocks before we came to the Wickland corner. From there I stuck to the waterfront streets until I came out near the marine supply store. It was dark as hell and a cold wind was blowing in off the bay. My beautiful, new medium weight topcoat was still in my apartment closet and the light covert job was feeling the pressure.

There was a light burning some place in the lame man's shop and I got an idea he might turn out to be of some use . . . the guy had a phone and he knew what I was after. I went around back and found the light. He lived in the back of the place from the looks of it. I located a door and rapped. The man's footsteps sounded, unevenly, to the door.

"Yes? Hello. It's you."

"Yeah. I've got a job to do down here and I may need some help."

"Come in. I've got coffee on."

The place smelled of the things that sort of place smells of: oakum, oils, and a kerosene stove. The coffee looked man-brewed as he poured out a cup and shoved me the canned milk. "I've located that boat for you, Mister."

"Good boy! That could save me getting shot at."

"Well, some of the fishing-boat boys were in. One of them is my brother—and I told him about it—confidentially, of course. When the other guys left, Sam, my brother, went back down and looked around. He knew the boat by sight and where she was tied up. Pretty soon he come back with her number. She ain't got any name on her transom, just a number on her bows. Federal regulation."

"What's her number?"

"He wrote it down. It's L . . . L . . . something. Here it is." He handed me the greasy slip of paper. "While he was there, sort of walkin' by minding his business like the rest of the fishing guys, he thought he seen a woman."

"He would have. More than likely." In figuring out how to get to the boat I got an idea. "Sam's a commercial fisherman, you say?"

"Commercial . . . and private parties. He does pretty well."

"I wonder if he'd like to make a few extra bucks—say fifty."

"He'd take it. What you got in mind?"

"These fellows at the Tea Wharf all tie up together, don't they?"

"That's right. One ties to the other. Sometimes you have to walk over half a dozen decks to get to your own boat."

"Then nobody expects a squawk when somebody noses in and makes fast to you, that right?"

"That's right. I get what you mean, too. Sam would hide you aboard and take you alongside them, or near, anyway."

"That's it. Can you get hold of him?"

"Sure. I can phone him at home. Fifty dollars, eh?"

In twenty minutes Sam turned up, a little redheaded guy with washed-out gray eyes that held a sort of tough humor. In twenty minutes more we'd started a big swing of the bay so as to approach the other side of the wharf as though we'd been outside in the open water. Sam had said maybe half a dozen words and asked nothing except what to do. When we began to ease off, as if looking for a place to tie up, I said:

"This might get rough, Sam."

He glanced back down the ladder where I was standing half in the cabin. I couldn't see his face. "I didn't figure you was paying fifty dollars for a three-mile joy ride, mister cop. Lenny told me about you."

As we nosed in, a man hollered, "Hi Sam! You're late!"

"I been callin', downbay."

"Why don't you marry the gal?"

"Maybe I will." I couldn't have staged it better if I'd written the script. Just another of the fishing boys coming home. We slowed to a gentle, rocking glide as we moved toward our objective. "Somebody stand by for a line, or can I come aboard?" And there it was. A fair-sized cruiser. Maybe forty feet. Not a light aboard. Just the riding light at the masthead. A man called, "Tie up down the line someplace, cap. We got to get out at daylight."

Sam hollered, "Okay, mac. There's a spot alongside here that'll leave you free." We edged along and Sam threw out a couple of fenders to keep us from scraping our target craft. In the cabin, I lost sight of everything. Nothing else was said as we made fast to the boat on the other side of us. I heard Sam's sneakers run forward and then felt the bow swing over as he warped her in to something solid like a piling. Finally he came back and shut off the idling motor and everything went terribly still—just the lapping of the restless bay, the occasional creak of the lines and the soft thump of the fenders. Sam turned off his running lights. I could see the green and red glow disappear from the cabin bulkhead.

Pretty soon the little redhead came down to the cabin and whispered close to my ear. "I'm goin' ashore . . . noisy, see?"

"Yeah. I understand. Thanks, Sam." I dug into my watch pocket where I'd stowed a folded fifty. "Here's your dough."

"Okay. I'll leave it with my brother. That's in case we get rolled or something."

"We?"

"Hell, yes. I'm goin' ashore . . . noisy, see? And then come back on the blind side, quiet."

"Oh. You're sure you want to? It may be a little rough—though, God knows, I don't want it that way." I'd be able to use a little company.

"Listen, pal, I found out I enjoy bein' scared. I'll be back."

I listened to him pound along the decks, singing his way to shore. A trail of growled protests followed him, but everybody in that friendly, accidental community took for granted who he was and where he was going.

There wasn't a sound from the boat alongside: the Maximilian H. Wardhouse of New York. I crawled flat on my belly across the deck and listened. A canopy above shielded me from the feeble glow of the riding light. I stuck my head beyond the cockpit combing and watched. They were not more than three or four feet away, our bow to their stern. They were headed out. Ready, I suppose, for a break. Leave at daylight, the voice had said—Maximilian's voice. Eddie would have until a little after five-thirty to get them on foot.

Then the Harbor Police. Then the Coast Guard. Keystone comedy. Only this was strictly not funny. I began to wonder what the hell I was doing there. I slipped off my shoes and my feet got cold—colder.

A match went up behind a curtained port on the boat across the way. Then out. In a minute or two I smelled cigarettes. Midge and Max weren't doing any sleeping. But they wouldn't have lit cigarettes if they'd been suspicious. After a while somebody pumped the head: "I can't get used to this damned thing." It was Midge. The guy said, "Shut up."

I was still listening hard when I heard a soft step behind me and I damned nearly scared myself to death. Sam groped around and touched me with his foot. I got up and went to the cabin. He said, "Notice what the tide's doin'? I thought of it when we tied up here."

I said I hadn't noticed. "The tide is turning, their bow line's fairly loose. They'll swing toward us. They'll be close in another half hour. We could step aboard."

I said, "What for?" Then I began to lay some plans. They were all based on the important premise that either or both of us would be insane to start any last-ditch scrap with a killer, maybe two killers. I had definitely placed both the man and the woman aboard—had, I was sure, recognized Midge Manson's voice. Eddie Marsh would be back before morning—at least he'd left word to that effect. I could send Sam to the hotel and get the cops—Harbor Police in case of a break and some of the Detective Bureau's run-of-the-mill strong-arm boys.

Sam seemed disappointed but agreed after a couple of vigorous counter-suggestions like sneaking aboard and jumping the pair of them. Again he took off, this time without sound. I went back to my cold post on my belly and stuck my head past the combing. The distance between the two boats was definitely narrowing. I could hear water dripping from their port bow line as it had lifted from the surface in tightening.

The tide brought a groan from our own lines, a thumping groan that might have been something else. I heard the man's voice, startlingly close, now.

"Listen!" A long silence. I listened, too, wondering what he'd heard. Then the man spoke again, a rough, hard whisper. "Listen!" More silence. "There's somebody aboard that boat."

"What boat? The one that came in?" It was Midge, barely audible.

"Yes. I heard something. There's somebody on there."

"The guy went away."

"Maybe he came back. Maybe he left somebody." I heard the man's heavy footstep in the cabin. "I'm gonna get the hell outta here. We've been tied up here too long. This thing can't last forever." Then Midge: "I've got to have a drink." More footsteps in the cabin. "Get me a drink while you're up." Midge and her liquor.

"Okay. But listen. What brains you got you're gonna need before we get across to Yarmouth Port. You start drinkin' heavy again and I'll kick your teeth in." He let that penetrate, then, "You know that, don't you?"

"Yeah. I know. Only right now I'm cold as hell and I need a drink. Gimme the bottle, will ya?"

I heard the squeak of a cork and a lot of silence. Pretty soon I caught another step or two. Then silence again. A moment later the deck under me made a strange movement, not the gentle and fairly well-established movement of the bay. I couldn't see anything in any direction but a gray, dull darkness through which the riding lights of a hundred small boats poked candle-fingers. I waited. Someone had stepped aboard us.

I crawled up into a knot and waited some more. I could have sworn, at one moment, that a darker place had appeared along-side the cabin bulkhead, a darker form which could have been a man standing on the scupper and holding the handrail. Then I knew it was a man, doing just that.

I crawled silently along the cockpit until I hit the transom seat. It was decked over in such a way that there was room beneath it for me to lie. I squeezed under. The man stepped from the rail into the cockpit. I heard his stocking feet scuff on the canvas, then stir the removable planking. I *felt* that. I was lying on the other end of the same boards. With as much economy of motion as I could, I hauled out my gun and held it in my left hand. I was lying on my right. The feet made a circuit of the cockpit, passed an inch from my head. I could feel his hands groping in front of him, hear them investigating the thwart seat over my head. I held my breath.

The steps continued around the rail and back to the companionway leading down to the cabin. The man slid the hatch back a little, very quietly. His shoulder brushed one of the hooks which are always fixed to each side of a cruiser hatch to hold it in place. The hook rattled and the man started down into the cabin. Halfway down the ladder he lit a flashlight and shot it ahead of him. I eased out from under the seat and crawled toward the companionway. I could see him moving forward.

I got to the hatch just about the time he was ready to turn back, satisfied that there was nobody aboard. On a second thought, he opened the door to the head and shot his light in. By the time he had turned, I'd slid the hatch into place and was closing the stout doors. He turned off his flash and made a run for it. The lock was in the hasp and open. I snapped it as he hit the panels. He started to bellow . . .

I said to shut up or I'd shoot him through the door.

He said, "Who are you?" I said, "Panty Burke!" The fellow hit the panel again, hard. It splintered a little and I put a shot through. He yelled and kept quiet. I didn't hear him fall. There was a step behind me . . .

The first thing I smelled was whisky. The first thing I felt was my head. It was quite natural that the first thing I thought was a hangover. Then I tried to move. My leg hurt like hell. I opened my eyes and there was no light. I raised my head and bumped it. I put out my arm and it bounced off a wall or something.

I tried to straighten myself out and found a coil or rope under me. Then things came together and I knew where I was. The reeling dizziness was only half in my head, the rest was in the unstable water under me. The roar was only half in my mind— the rest in that Packard engine. I was in the lazaret of Midge Manson's boat, headed for Yarmouth Port. That is, the boat was headed for Yarmouth Port. It was pretty certain I wouldn't get that far.

I felt under my left trousers leg down along the shin. There was a hell of a swelling near the ankle. I damned nearly went out again when I touched it. The whisky didn't seem to be on my breath but it was all over my clothes. There was a throbbing lump over my right ear and I figured Midge had hit me with a whisky bottle. Last I'd heard her, she had one in her hand. I guess I was too sick to be scared.

I couldn't figure out how long I'd been knocked out, but I could get some idea of how far out to sea we'd gone because of the big, rough ground swell which plagues the bay most of the time. I reached up and felt a glass port and knew it was still dark. The engine pounded along.

After a while somebody opened the doors and said, "Come out." It was the guy. And he wasn't inviting me to waltz. I slid out on my seat, feet first, into the dim light of the cabin. The bunks were down and empty. I dragged myself up onto one of them and sat. The guy had a gun in his hand and he sat down opposite. I'd never seen him before. He didn't look like much of anything to describe, just tough.

I said, "I need a drink." He got up and went to a rack for a whisky bottle. Handed it to me. I took a long pull, came up for breath, and took another. The guy took the bottle back and put it beside him on the bunk.

"Now you better talk, Doc."

I thought it over a little, expecting to get clouted. The man across the cabin didn't move. My leg was making me faint and sick. Yes, I had to talk to this guy or else. It didn't make any difference one way or the other. He knew the facts. What he didn't know was how much the police had found out. That would be important to him.

I said, "Yeah. I guess I'd better."

He stared at me. I watched the sweat seep out on his face. The cabin was stuffy but it wasn't hot. I was pretty frightened. I'm not always scared of a tough guy, but I'm terrified by a desperate one. This guy was the works and I knew it. He held the gun in his fist and waited.

I said, "Give me another drink. I've got a broken leg." He held the bottle to me.

"You fell down the companionway."

I took another drink and put the bottle down on my bunk, far enough away so I couldn't have used it for a weapon. The man started to reach for it, grunted and left it there. I started to talk. Why not?

"I'll tell you. There isn't a hell of a lot to say. I know all of it, now. I just got back from Middle Fairfield and I've identified the x-rays. I found the safety-deposit keys and got Stirnie Maize to open the box . . ."

"You read the agreement, then."

"Yes. I read the agreement."

"Then what brought you here?"

"A set of 1939 Packard manifold gaskets."

"Smart bastard, aren't you!"

"I wouldn't be here if I was smart."

The guy looked at me with a funny expression on his face. It made me sicker than I felt already. "You wouldn't be here if I was smart, myself, neither would I. I guess you know how bad it is."

"I know. I've got only one out, that's to show you how bad it really is. The police know everything I know, you understand."

"I didn't, but I'll believe you."

"You haven't got a chance."

He gave me that look again and said, "Neither have you."

"Why add another killing when you can't win?" I put all I had in it. "You'll be better off when they take you if I'm all in one piece."

"I'm not that kind of a guy, Doc. I'll go for all of it." He looked at the gun. "Yeah. I'll go for the roll. Tell me. You might as well. How much did Grace Larkin know?"

"As a matter of fact, Grace Larkin didn't know anything. She told the cops a lot of stuff, but none of it . . ."

There was a violent wrenching of the boat and a small scream aft. I was thrown forward on my broken leg and probably yelled, myself. The man jumped up and said, "What the hell!"

Midge Manson hollered something and I looked up the companionway in time to see a glare of white light catch and hold the cockpit. The woman yelled, "Get up here, quick! Somebody's got a light on us!" The boat rolled desperately in the other direction and I bounced back into the bunk. A siren sounded over the water and somebody off someplace fired a shot. The guy stumbled against me and lurched toward the ladder. He yelled, "Gimme that wheel. Get down there and watch him—he'll start something."

I watched up through the hatch for Midge to appear. The blazing white light still poured on as we wheeled and plunged for cover. Then the woman came down, her face dirty, mottled gray and her eyes blazing hatred. She stopped at the foot of the ladder and hung on.

"You did this to us. You. You did it to us, you lousy cop-lover!" She edged her way to the bunk on the other side of the cabin. She had nothing in her hands. They must have had only one gun between them and the man on deck was firing that, probably at the light.

Midge reached across and picked up the whisky bottle. She moved aft again away from me, took the cork out and swigged a lot of it, keeping one eye on me. It must have looked funny but I was sick as hell and my leg made me sweat. I heard some shouting off someplace.

"You . . . stinkin' cop-lover!" She drooled with fear and whisky. "I hit you with one of these already tonight. Next time I'm going to make it stick."

Somehow I had to hold out. I felt myself slipping away and had to struggle back through pain again. I fought against comfort to bring myself back to agony. Hard to do.

The shooting outside sorted itself out—almost all of it was coming from another boat. A megaphoned shout boomed in. It seemed close. "Heave to, there! You're under arrest!"

The guy on deck answered with a couple of shots and swung off on a sharp angle. I looked up and saw the light leave us, heard a powerful motor roar by astern. The engine snarled as our wheel came out of the water. We bucked a couple of hard swells and steadied out on a new course.

Then the light hit us again and there was a quick burst of submachine-gun fire. Slugs pounded like sledges into the hull. The man in the cockpit screamed and the boat veered off hard. It hurt my leg. I vomited on the deck. I made it quick for fear the woman would brain me.

Something hit us alongside and I heard shouts—hard pounding, stumbling footsteps. I looked up and Midge Manson was standing in front of me with the bottle in her hand.

Eddie Marsh's voice roared down the companionway. "Shut off that engine, somebody. This one's out. Cuff him. It's Burke. I've got his gun."

The woman raised the bottle. I remember her mouth. It was loose and maniacal. I slapped the thing out of her hand. She stood there. I got partly up on my good leg, gave her a little shove away from me. I heard Eddie's voice again, closer this time, he must have been standing in the companionway . . .

"Doc!" His roar filled the place and I knew I could pass out if I had to. "Doc! Are you all right?"

Then the woman charged. I knew I had to hit her. I swung a sharp right hand at the point of her jaw—I had to. I've never hit a woman and, even then, it seemed shameful. But I swung hard.

She moved her head to one side and I missed. I saw her left fist come flashing up inside my right shoulder but I couldn't get away from it. I fell forward onto the deck.

I remember something—the last thing that filtered through that nightmare of pain and blear. It was something about Eddie Marsh.

I think the son of a bitch laughed.

21

I dreamed of confusion and pain—disorderly shouting from somewhere above and a nasty, heaving piece of linoleum below, pressing violently against me at odd, sickening intervals. I pulled my head off the deck and reorientated myself, one dull thought after another.

The cabin was deserted. The drooling witch had been dragged off somewhere without her bottle. I crawled to it and drank out of it. The cushioned bunks were too far away and I stayed on the deck.

The shouting organized itself into words with meaning. The police boat was lashing us alongside, bumping us with big, shuddering jolts that I felt mostly in my leg.

Eddie Marsh and another guy came down the ladder in slickers. I felt Eddie's hands touch me and heard his voice.

"It's all over, Doc. Take it easy."

His wet-rubber arms went under me and I was on the bunk. I guess I yelled a little when my leg swung free because he said:

"What's the matter, kid? What did they do to you?"

I must have told him because the other guy started cutting off the leg of my pants. I decided to pass out again for a while and let go. When I began to pay attention again I had an ice-pack on my leg and a morphinous warmth in my system. As a matter of fact, it all seemed very jolly. The big motors alongside us were still running but we didn't seem to be heaving about. Eddie was sitting across from me looking worried in a heavy sort of way. His old brown hat had replaced the sou'wester and his blue suit looked more wrinkled than ever. Altogether he looked pretty silly and I told him so.

"You don't look too hot yourself. How do you feel?"

I told him I felt wonderful and where the hell were we?

"About ten minutes out. The thing's all wound up. I haven't asked for any statements yet, but we'll get 'em soon enough. The woman was too drunk to make any sense and I winged Burke pretty badly . . ."

"You winged who?"

"Burke." The big stupe didn't even question it. "He's not critically hurt but we gave him a shot of . . ."

I couldn't stop laughing. It hurt like fire and made me nauseated, and still I laughed. Eddie must have sat there burning but I couldn't see him.

"What's funny?"

I guess it was the morphine, maybe the whisky.

"Hey! Quit that! What's so goddam funny?"

Poor Eddie—with his teletype reports, his fingerprints, with his wonderful, forthright way of ploughing straight through to the end. He'd have had these people, come hell or high water, sooner or later. I guess he thought I was hysterical because he sat over beside me and held my hand. It was all right, too. It felt sure and strong and warm with the things that had made us, and kept us, friends. I stopped laughing.

"The man you shot wasn't Burke, Eddie." I made it as gentle as I could.

"Wasn't Burke? I don't get you." He was completely thrown for a loss. "If he wasn't Burke, who was he . . . and where's Burke."

"He was Pike Manson. Burke's been dead since the start."

"That's impossible. You're dopey. Grace Larkin showed me those prints you got, on the gasket. Burke's."

"That's the whole deal, Eddie. That was the gimmick. Burke was murdered somewhere around October eighteenth. The police of Middle Fairfield did the rest for you. They sent Burke's prints to Washington all carefully tagged with Manson's name. From there on it all got wrong. Actually it's very simple, once you know that. Just trade prints in your mind and your case is straightaway."

"But the stuff in Burke's ventilator . . ."

"Maximilian Wardhouse."

"What?"

"Manson, registered under any name he could think of, in that interval before you looked for Burke, in that three weeks. He could have even done it before that."

"What about your prints on the razor—the ones you found in Grace Larkin's bathroom?"

"You called them Manson's. They were Burke's, of course."

"Don't say 'of course' like that. It irritates me."

"Okay. I couldn't have said it yesterday."

"Did you know Manson when you saw him?"

"No. I'd never seen either of them before, any more than you had. They aren't unlike physically, although that's not important at all. No. I didn't know them any more than you did."

"I see." The fellow shook his head a couple of times as if to shake off the impossibility of the whole thing. "Then the prints at the Peters' killing . . . yes. I see."

"That's it. Manson's were fresh and on the *outside* of the metal box. Burke's were old and on the inside. Old records. We simply had them backwards."

"That way you have to swap motives, too."

"Right . . . and plenty of motive. Start with several thousand dollars in cash, add the one threat to Manson's comparatively safe pursuit of his counterfeiting business with Peters, add a perfectly sound fall-guy in the person of Burke to take all the charges and top it off with a big shot of personal venom. Lots of motive."

"Yeah. It would seem that way." From someplace inside he dug up his old black book, looked at it with some feeling. "Simple, wasn't it!"

"It seems simple now. They did some foolish things."

Eddie sighed. "I suppose so. They always do. You don't find that out until you catch up with them, unfortunately." The big guy put away his book. "So Manson runs around New York stealing groceries—they're right here in the lockers—and practically gets off to Yarmouth Port, all directly under our noses."

"I don't suppose he showed himself much, but that's just about what he did." I cast back over the thing in my mind. "Midge, of course, was the plotter, native to her. She's cruel and devious, and smart."

"She's in it all the way, then . . ."

"She killed Burke, if that's what you mean."

"How?" Eddie was thinking of the Middle Fairfield police.

"In as nasty a way as anybody was ever killed. It took special knowledge and the confidence of the devil. I don't know all about it yet, but I know the over-all method. I'd like to hear her confession—it'll be a great story when we get it."

There were some voices above and we slowed down. Eddie got up and stood there a second, staring at me. "We'll get it."

I let go again and wished for another shot of morphine. In thirty seconds the young ambulance guy was there with it.

I went to sleep somewhere along the way because ambulances are very soothing and the siren dulcet and the passing lights play pleasantly on the walls . . .

I went to sleep thinking that Katie would be up ahead there someplace with a New Year's horn and a paper cap.

But I didn't go to sleep without wondering why they let people like Grace Larkin hit bottom so hard—and stay there so long.

The nurse's name was Casey. She pulled up the shades and starched around the room until I woke up. She slapped a thermometer into my mouth and said good morning. Then she breezed out of the place and thumped down the hall. I waited until I got bored with the thermometer and stuck it on the bed table. With my right foot, I experimented with my cast. It seemed too damned long and heavy. Through the open door I could see people going by, more cops than anybody. I heard the nurse coming back and shoved the thermometer in my mouth again. Casey read it, looked at me and said:

"I'll get the heating pads immediately. I'll get lots of them. I'm certain you'll feel better, Doctor."

"What are you talking about?"

"Your temperature is sixty-one." She shook the thing down again. "Perhaps you'd like to try it again, just to make sure?"

While I was in the silence, Eddie Marsh walked in and said good morning.

"The doctor says you can go back to New York any time you feel like it—the sooner the better, as a matter of fact, because he wants traction on that break."

"Well, I damned well don't want traction on it. I want to hobble around on crutches like anybody else with a broken ankle." Traction! Damn these overeducated veterinarians!

Casey said, "He's probably got a date to dance tonight. It's New Year's Eve after all."

I said something like "New Year's Eve . . . Omigod, Katie!" Eddie cheerfully announced that he'd called Katie and that she was looking for a hospital bed for my apartment. It was all settled, it seemed. New Year's Eve. I'd get home today, or else.

Eddie spoke up. "I've got a drawing room on the two-o'clock if that's all right with you. We're taking the Mansons back, in a separate compartment if that makes you nervous."

"Quiet! Yes, if you can't make it sooner. Have they talked?"

"Manson's still pretty much out but the woman's been trying to tell me things all night. I wouldn't take a statement from her until you were able to hear it. She'll talk any time. Feel up to it?"

"Sure. When?" I wanted to hear Midge Manson's story worse than a cat ever wanted kittens.

"Right now, if you'd like. She's just across the hall. There'll be a couple of others, of course—a stenographer and one or two of the Boston men who've helped . . ."

I said to bring them in and the nurse beat it. I felt a little wave of disgust at the prospect of sitting in on the end of a life and that's what it was. Not the end of a kid game of run-sheep-run where everybody gets together and admits where he's been during the chase. It was the end of the road for a mean, hard soul who tried to make things come out her way instead of the way they had to be.

A cop in uniform came in and put a notebook on the table by the windows. A couple of others, in plain clothes, brought extra chairs. Then Midge Manson walked in. Marsh was behind her. She looked at me and said, "Hello, Doc." One of the guys indicated the armchair and she sat down. Eddie closed the door and moved across the room. He was very serious.

"Mrs. Manson, I think you know, from what we've told you, that we have secured all the evidence necessary to prove that you and your husband killed William Edward Burke." Midge sat staring at the floor and said nothing. "You have indicated to me and to these officers, Captain Flynn and Sergeant Bettina that you wish to make a statement. Is that correct?"

"That's right."

"Do you understand that you are not forced to make such a statement and that it may, at some time, be brought as evidence against you?"

"Yes." Her voice was very low.

"Very well." Eddie sat down. "What's your name?" From there it went on, steadily and in a droning, mechanical detail that was ugly and tiresome. She had been a nurse. She had been in show business, afterward, in a small way. She had met Manson at the racetrack and married him. On and on.

Burke had been too strong for Manson. Manson had hated him from the start. Midge had hated both of them . . .

"Pike was stupid. He let Burke take all the play away from him. Burke wouldn't take a fast dollar, wouldn't open up. Manson is just dumb—dumb and tough."

"When did you plan to kill Burke?" Midge didn't even look up.

"Before we went to Boston. He and Pike had been having trouble over . . . over some things Pike wanted to do. And Burke made Pike sign a statement . . ."

It was all pretty much as I'd figured it out. Money, distrust and hatred, backed up by a supposedly foolproof plan for getting rid of Burke. It seems that Midge had got the idea while she was working in a drying-out spot for alcoholics in Florida. Then they came to it:

Eddie said, "Just how did you kill Burke?"

The listlessness went out of the woman and she smiled—looked up at me and said, "You don't know yet, do you, Doc!"

I said no and that I'd never heard of anything so ingenious and how in the world did she ever think of it, or something like that. From then on it was run-sheep-run. Midge rushed happily into her horrible tale as though there was a prize waiting for her instead of a shaved head and brine-soaked electrodes.

"Pike did all the heavy stuff. He's good at that. He went into the station and caught Burke looking for a porter. He stuck a gun in the guy's ribs and said he wanted to talk to him once more before Burke left for Florida. We had a car, then, and Pike walked Burke out to Eighth Avenue and made him get in. I was driving. The men sat in the back and we took off for the West Side highway. Burke got tough and Pike sapped him. From there on Pike drove and I took over."

I said, "Pike had knocked him out?" She smiled like a kid with a cone.

"You ought to know, Doc."

"Yeah. Grace Larkin, too."

She said, "I didn't like that." Then she went on. "From there on I took over. Burke was never conscious again . . ."

Eddie leaned forward. "I don't understand . . ." The woman snapped back at him. "You wouldn't, not you. Doc will, though. Burke never knew anything from the time Pike sapped him until three days later when he died. That's hard to do—know it, Doc?"

"Without killing the guy outright, yes. How'd you do it?"

"First it was ether, not much but steady. I got him on the floor of the car and we kept going. Ether, Doc, then I gave him the old 'Panty, Panty, what in the world happened to you? Here, drink this.' That was the whisky and barbiturate. That lasted most of the way to Boston. I got him the rest of the way on one healthy hypodermic shot of morphia. Neat, Doc?"

I said for her to get on with it, that the rest of it was the neat part.

"We had a basement apartment then, down the street from where I've been living since. The garages were in back and he was no trouble. That night I mailed a letter to the Middle Fair-field cops and one to Pike care of General Delivery there. You ran across them, I guess . . ."

I said we had.

"That night, too, I started the intravenous alcohol—in the foot so I could cover it up—never too much—never enough to damage tissue. Just right, Doc. I watched his pulse rate. Pike went over to Middle Fairfield and sized up the spot. He collected the letter and was careful to blow a whisky breath at the clerk. I figured that out, too. We cooked up the scenery together. He'd be just another bum trying to keep warm along the tracks. We carried that prop fire over in a bucket."

Eddie muttered something under his breath.

"Three days later, the eighteenth, I knew he was about gone. His pulse was too fast and too irregular to count and he wasn't breathing good. I wanted him in Middle Fairfield during that night and it was ninety miles. I stepped up the alcohol and ster-ile water and he died about twenty minutes later. We took him to the car—I'd squawked to the neighbors about Pike's boozing and we'd staged a couple of mild brawls. Nobody would have said anything if they'd seen us. But they didn't."

Eddie made another noise in his throat.

"We put him in the car and set out . . ."

I couldn't take any more and said, "Get that thing out of my room, will you, Eddie? I've had enough."

Eddie said, "So have I."

Midge Manson said, "What's the matter, boys? Goin' soft?"

L'ENVOI

"And," said Katie, "when we've finished this *Jungle Book*, there's always the other one to look forward to. Kipling wrote two, you know."

New Year's Eve roared in from Broadway with horns, whistles and bells. People were singing down there. People without broken legs. New Year's Eve, and I was being read the *Jungle Book!* It was definitely time for a beef.

"Look, Katie, my darlin', I don't want to seem unappreciative but . . . I mean, after all, it is the gayest night of the year . . . and, well *Jungle Books* . . ."

"You haven't ever read them, have you?"

"No."

"Nor *With Henty in Darkest Africa?*"

"No . . . but . . ."

"Nor *Treasure Island?*"

"I think I started that. I can't see . . ."

"Well, I'll tell you. All the authorities agree. I looked it up. If you had read that sort of thing when you were young, or even if they'd had radio serials, you wouldn't be running off on those silly, adolescent adventures with Eddie Marsh at your age. Breaking your leg and everything."

"But New Year's Eve, darling! After all there is champagne in the refrigerator. Left over from Christmas . . ."

"There is?" A quality of hesitancy in her voice gave me hope. "I'd forgotten. Perhaps we *could* have a little champagne."

I said bravo or something and loved her desperately as she clattered about in the kitchen. She brought two glasses and a well-chilled quart which I opened silently, as in the best places.

Times Square screamed, suddenly, that it was midnight and we said Happy New Year and bottoms up, and things. The queen-of-love-and-beauty gave me a possessive kiss and a considerable lecture about threshing around with my leg in a traction splint. All in all, I was about as happy as guys ever get.

We had another toast and then Katie sat back in her big chair, beaming like your maiden aunt at commencement, and began:

"Now *this* is the story of Rikki Tikki Tavi . . ."

Print-on-demand titles available at
CoachwhipBooks.com

Ebook titles available at
Coachwhip.com

ODDS-ON MURDER

DANCE

JACK DOLPH

Jack Dolph

MURDER
MAKES
THE MARE GO

hot tip JACK DOLPH

TIP SHEET
DAILY RATINGS

JACK DOLPH

DEAD ANGEL

A.M. JAOSS

ANITA BOUTELL

DEATH BRINGS
A STORKE

CRADLED
IN FEAR

ANONYMOUS FOOTSTEPS | JOHN. M. O'CONNOR

THE
RUMBLE
MURDERS

Henry Ware Eliot, Jr.

SHOW
BUSINESS

A FAST-MOVING MYSTERY BY
BRYANT FORD

THE
BEACON HILL
MURDERS

THE
BACK BAY
MURDERS

THE ROGER SCARLETT MYSTERIES
VOL. 1

CAT'S PAW

MURDER
AMONG THE
ANGELLS

THE ROGER SCARLETT MYSTERIES
VOL. 2

IN THE
FIRST
DEGREE

THE ROGER SCARLETT MYSTERIES
VOL. 3

SAMUEL ROGERS

YOU'LL BE
SORRY!

YOU LEAVE
ME COLD!

MURDER
IN BERMUDA

WILLOUGHBY SHARP

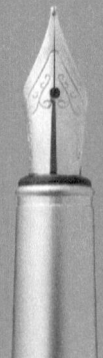

MURDER OF
THE HONEST BROKER

WILLOUGHBY SHARP

THE SERGEANT HARTY MYSTERIES
JOEL Y. DANE

MURDER CUM LAUDE
— ① —
THE CABANA MURDERS

THE SERGEANT HARTY MYSTERIES
JOEL Y. DANE

GRASP AT STRAWS
— ② —
THE CHRISTMAS TREE MURDERS

LOUIS F. BOOTH

THE BANK VAULT MYSTERY

BROKERS' END

A
Matter of
Iodine

David Keith

THE
DARTMOUTH
MURDERS

THE
WAILING ROCK
MURDERS

CLIFFORD
ORR

MOST MEN DON'T KILL

MURDER IN BLACK AND WHITE

DAVID ALEXANDER

www.ingramcontent.com/pod-product-compliance
Lightning Source LLC
Chambersburg PA
CBHW030501260626

47157CB00005B/1597